Everyman, I will go with thee,
and be thy guide

THE EVERYMAN LIBRARY

The Everyman Library was founded by J. M. Dent in 1906. He chose the name Everyman because he wanted to make available the best books ever written in every field to the greatest number of people at the cheapest possible price. He began with Boswell's 'Life of Johnson'; his one-thousandth title was Aristotle's 'Metaphysics', by which time sales exceeded forty million.

Today Everyman paperbacks remain true to J. M. Dent's aims and high standards, with a wide range of titles at affordable prices in editions which address the needs of today's readers. Each new text is reset to give a clear, elegant page and to incorporate the latest thinking and scholarship. Each book carries the pilgrim logo, the character in 'Everyman', a medieval mystery play, a proud link between Everyman past and present.

Alexander Pushkin

YEVGENY ONEGIN

Edited, with revised translation, by

A. D. P. BRIGGS

University of Birmingham

Based on a translation by

OLIVER ELTON

Illustrated by

M. V. DOBUJINSKY

EVERYMAN

J. M. DENT • LONDON

CHARLES E. TUTTLE

VERMONT

A. D. P. Briggs is Consultant Editor
for the Everyman Russian Series

First published in Everyman in 1995

J. M. Dent
Orion Publishing Group
Orion House
5 Upper St Martin's Lane
London WC2H 9EA
and
Charles E. Tuttle Co. Inc.
28 South Main Street
Rutland, Vermont 05701, USA

Typeset by CentraCet Ltd
Printed in Great Britain by
The Guernsey Press Co. Ltd, Guernsey, C.I.

British Library Cataloguing-in-Publication Data
is available upon request.

ISBN 0 460 87595 7

CONTENTS

NOTE ON THE AUTHOR AND EDITOR

ALEKSANDR SERGEYEVICH PUSHKIN was born in Moscow on 26 May 1799. After studying at the new lycée of Tsarskoye Selo, near St Petersburg (1811–17), he took up an undemanding government position and indulged in a dissipated lifestyle, maintaining tenuous links with revolutionary-minded young people. In 1820 he finished his first long poem, *Ruslan and Lyudmila*, but was exiled the same year to Yekaterinoslav in the far south, moving to Kishinev, the capital of Bessarabia, before the end of the year. *The Captive in the Caucasus* and *The Fountain of Bakhchisaray* were written in 1820–22 and on 9 May 1823 he began *Yevgeny Onegin*. Allowed to return north, he remained in exile on his home estate at Mikhaylovskoye during 1824–5; this is the period of *The Gypsies*, *Count Nulin* and the Shakespearean play, *Boris Godunov*. On 8 September 1825 he was summoned to Moscow, where the tsar, Nicholas I, became his personal censor. His earlier dissipated lifestyle was resumed. During 1829 he paid a long visit to Transcaucasia and saw action in the war against Turkey. Stranded at his new estate of Boldino in September 1830, he wrote prolifically for three months, producing *The Little House in Kolomna*, four *Little Tragedies* (including *Mozart and Salieri*) and the five *Tales of Belkin* (in prose). He married Natalya Goncharova in 1831 and, on 5 October of that year, he completed *Yevgeny Onegin*, having worked on it for more than eight years. A long journey to the Urals in 1833 provided him with material for his historical tale, *The Captain's Daughter* (1833–5). Two unhappy years in St Petersburg (1834–6) brought him humiliation in court circles and mounting debts; suffering also from jealousy of his wife's admirers, he did little creative work. Finally he was goaded by scandalous rumours into a duel with Georges D'Anthès, an adopted son of the Dutch ambassador. The duel took place on 27 January 1837. Pushkin was wounded in the stomach and died two days later. Universally acknowledged as Russia's greatest poet, Pushkin set the standards and provided models which have formed and directed the national literature ever since. The Russian language itself was reformed by his innovatory use of it. His 800 lyrics, numerous narrative poems, dramatic works, tales in verse and prose, historical and critical articles, along with his collected letters, comprise the richest single treasure-house in Russian culture. His works have inspired thousands of musical versions, including several famous operas.

A. D. P. BRIGGS, Professor of Russian Language and Literature at the University of Birmingham, is a specialist in modern Russian literature, mainly of the nineteenth century. Among his many publications are six books, three of them devoted to Alexander Pushkin. His current work is on Pushkin and music.

CHRONOLOGY OF PUSHKIN'S LIFE

Year	*Age*	*Life*
1799		26 May: Born in Moscow
1800–11	1–11	Grows up without parental affection, entrusted to nursemaids, French tutors and governesses. Lazy, but an avid, precocious reader. Learns Russian from household serfs and especially his nanny, Arina Rodionovna

CHRONOLOGY OF HIS TIMES

Year	*Artistic Events*	*Historical Events*
1798		Napoleon captures Malta and invades Egypt French fleet defeated by Nelson at Battle of the Nile
1799	Birth of Balzac	French occupy Naples and Zurich Napoleon defeats Turks; made First Consul Death of George Washington
1800		Austrians defeated by Napoleon at Marengo
1801	Chateaubriand, *Atala*	Murder of Tsar Paul; accession of Alexander I
1802	Death of Radishchev, author of *A Journey from St Petersburg to Moscow* Birth of Hugo Mme de Staël, *Delphine* Chateaubriand, *René*	Napoleon made First Consul for life France annexes Piedmont
1803	Death of Bogdanovich, poet, author of *Dushen'ka*	Great Britain declares war against France
1804	Birth of George Sand Death of Kant	Napoleon becomes Emperor
1805	Death of Schiller	Battles of Trafalgar and Austerlitz
1806		Battle of Jena; Napoleon occupies Berlin
1807	Mme de Staël, *Corinne*	Battle of Friedland; Russians defeated by Napoleon
1808	Scott, *Marmion* Goethe, *Faust*, Part One	Napoleon enters Rome Wellington enters Spain Siege of Saragossa
1809	Birth of Gogol Krylov, first book of fables	Battle of Corunna; death of Sir John Moore

Year	*Age*	*Life*
1811–17	11–17	Studies at the new lycée of Tsarskoye Selo, near St Petersburg
1817–20	17–20	Undemanding government post in St Petersburg. Dissipated life style; some links with revolutionary young people. Some unpublishable liberal poems circulate in manuscript

Year	*Artistic Events*	*Historical Events*
1810	Birth of Musset Mme de Staël, *De l'Allemagne*	France annexes Holland
1811	Zhukovsky, *Svetlana* Austen, *Sense and Sensibility* Byron, *Childe Harold's Pilgrimage*, Cantos One and Two Birth of Belinsky, radical literary critic	
1812		Napoleon declares war on Russia; battle of Borodino French defeat Russians; burning of Moscow, followed by Napoleon's retreat
1813	Austen, *Pride and Prejudice* Byron, *The Giaour*	Wellington invades France
1814	Birth of Lermontov Scott, *Waverley*	Allied sovereigns enter Paris Napoleon deposed, banished to Elba
1815		British defeated at Battle of New Orleans Napoleon returns to Paris Defeat of Napoleon at Battle of Waterloo Allies enter Paris Napoleon sent to St Helena
1816	Deaths of the poet Derzhavin and dramatist Ozerov Byron, *The Prisoner of Chillon* Coleridge, *Christabel* Constant, *Adolphe* Goethe, *Italienische Reise*	
1817	Byron, *Manfred* and remainder of *Childe Harold's Pilgrimage*	
1818	Birth of Turgenev Death of satirical journalist, Novikov Byron, *Beppo*	
1819	Byron, *Don Juan*, Cantos One and Two Stendhal, *De l'Amour*	Florida ceded to USA by Spain Birth of future Queen Victoria

Year	*Age*	*Life*
1820	20	*Ruslan and Lyudmila*. Exiled to Yekaterinoslav; transferred to Kishinev
1821	21	*The Captive in the Caucasus*, *The Robber Brothers*
1822	22	*The Fountain of Bakhchisaray*
1823	23	Begins *Yevgeny Onegin*. Transferred to Odessa
1824	24	Returns north to internal exile at Mikhaylovskoye. *The Gypsies*
1825	25	*Count Nulin*, *Boris Godunov*. Freed from exile, but with Nicholas I as personal censor in Moscow
1828	28	*Poltava*
1829	29	Visits Transcaucasia; action against the Turks
1830	30	Stranded at Boldino by cholera outbreak. *The Little House in Kolomna*, *Little Tragedies*, *Tales of Belkin*
1831	31	18 February: marries Natalya Goncharova. 5 October: completes *Yevgeny Onegin*
1833	33	Travels east to the Urals, engaged in historical research. Second 'Boldino Autumn'. *Andzhelo*, *The Bronze Horseman*, *The Queen of Spades*
1833–5	33–5	*The Captain's Daughter*
1833–6	33–6	Unhappy period in St Petersburg. Humiliation in court circles, mounting debts, jealousy of wife's admirers. Little creative work done
1837	37	Goaded by scandalous rumours into a duel with Georges D'Anthès, adopted son of Dutch ambassador. 27 January: Pushkin wounded in the stomach in duel with D'Anthès; dies two days later

Year	Artistic Events	Historical Events
1820	Lamartine, *Premières Méditations* Shelley, *Prometheus Unbound*	Naples; Carbonari revolt
1821	Births of Dostoyevsky, Baudelaire and Flaubert Death of Keats	Austrians occupy Naples Death of Napoleon
1822	Death of Shelley	Greek Declaration of Independence
1823	Lamartine, *Nouvelles Méditations*	French invade Spain
1824	Byron, remainder of *Don Juan* Death of Byron Griboyedov, *Woe from Wit*	
1825	Death of poet and revolutionary Ryleyev (executed) Death of Karamzin	Death of Alexander I; accession of Nicholas I Ruthless suppression of Decembrist uprising
1827	Death of Blake Manzoni, *I Promessi Sposi*	Kingdom of Greece founded
1828	Birth of Leo Tolstoy	Russia declares war against Turkey
1829	Death of Griboyedov Balzac, *Les Chouans*	Andrew Jackson US President
1830	Battle of *Hernani*	Death of George IV; accession of William IV Louis Philippe proclaimed King of France
1831	Death of Hegel Stendhal, *Le Rouge et le Noir*	Poles defeat Russians at Grochow
1832	Goethe, *Faust*, Part Two Deaths of Goethe and Scott	Poland annexed by Russia
1833	Heine, *Die romantische Schule*	Slavery abolished in British colonies
1834	Death of Coleridge	
1837		Death of William IV; accession of Queen Victoria

INTRODUCTION

A Russian Masterpiece in Context

In less than two centuries Russian literature has made a tremendous contribution to European culture. The names of Dostoyevsky, Tolstoy, Turgenev, Gogol, Chekhov, Gorky, Sholokhov, Pasternak and Solzhenitsyn – to parade only some of those most familiar to western readers – resound with a significance and popularity which cannot be ignored. These Russian writers are accompanied by dozens of others in many ways hardly less accomplished; a literary collective amounting to a great national dynasty. All of its members are intimately related through mutual respect and multiple cross-reference, in a manner difficult to comprehend by outsiders. Adept at story-telling, sensitive to form and full of imaginative originality, they have mastered all the literary arts. They have also probed and extended our understanding of reality by asking serious questions about human society, psychology and philosophy. They have provided inspiration for artists beyond the writing community, particularly the many Russian composers who rival them in appeal and reputation. The father of them all, with no close rival for the title of Russia's greatest poet, is Alexander Pushkin. The greatest of his works is *Yevgeny Onegin*.[1]

Pushkin lived for only thirty-seven years (1799–1837), but he left behind a prolific legacy extending over many literary genres, with a masterpiece in each one of them. He set standards and provided models which have formed and directed both the Russian language and the national literature from his death to the present day. A dozen narrative poems; over eight hundred lyrics of every imaginable kind; a full-length Shakespearean history-play, *Boris Godunov*, together with several miniature dramas (the *Little Tragedies*, including *Mozart and Salieri*); a

[1] For an explanation of the spelling of this name see the *Note on the Text*, pp. xxviii–xxix.

short prose novel, *The Captain's Daughter* and several stories including *The Queen of Spades*; voluminous critical, historical and epistolary prose – all of this constitutes his great gift to the Russian nation, a treasure-house without equal. To compare Pushkin with Mozart, as many have done, is helpful. Both artists represent the culmination of a classical age, which ensures the profoundest respect for formal perfection; both anticipate the nineteenth century, however, with a rich display of originality and imagination. In both of them we encounter an irrepressible and spontaneous flow of melodic inventiveness which appears to be effortless but actually depended upon much revision and straightforward hard work; in each case apparent simplicity disguises both intricacy and profundity, while a paradoxical sense of lightness and carefree enjoyment is mixed poignantly with an awareness of human unhappiness. Both pretend to a casual manner, but actually touch upon deep seriousness and sometimes tragedy.

Pushkin's novel in verse, *Yevgeny Onegin*, occupied its author for more than eight years (1823–31). It is quite short for a novel, consisting of not much more than 20,000 words. (To take a roughly contemporary example from the early Victorian period of English literature, Charles Dickens's *A Christmas Carol* (1843), is half as long again and *David Copperfield* is at least twelve times as long.) Pushkin's brevity is no deficiency; it does not diminish the work in terms of its comprehensive coverage of character and incident or its seriousness. The gifted poet can say in fifty words as much as many an expansive novelist in half a chapter. (Alan Bennett makes this point with memorable clumsiness in a diary entry which says, 'Poetry is supreme, because it makes less mess.') Poetry is the first, and greatest, quality of *Yevgeny Onegin*, but to appreciate this fully a sound knowledge of Russian is needed. Nevertheless, there is much to be gained from reading the novel in translation. Before deciding what this is, it is necessary to say a few words about the two languages involved and the unavoidable difficulties encountered in translation from one to the other.

Problems of Translation

Russian and English, distant cousins in the Indo-European family of languages, have certain similarities, certain differences.

What brings them close together is the impressive energy generated by clear vowels, powerful consonants and strong word stress, all of this linked to a demotic willingness, over the centuries, to absorb vocabulary on a massive scale from outside. (In this regard, French, with its nasal tones, stresslessness and patrician sense of superiority, fending off all importations, resembles neither of them). Thus the task of translating Russian poetry into English *begins* with some advantages, which soon dissolve.

Where Russian and English depart from each other most noticeably is in the matter of word-length. This may be illustrated by examining two very different kinds of English poetry. On the one hand, our language can do a great deal with short and snappy expressions. Extreme cases may be seen in Fitzgerald's aphoristic injunction, 'Drink! for you know not whence you came nor why: / Drink! for you know not why you go nor where' (*Rubaiyat of Omar Khayyam*), or in Sylvia Plath's lovely poem about childbirth, *A Thing So Clear*, in which she says of her new-born son, 'His lids are like the lilac flower / And soft as a moth his breath. / I shall not let go. / There is no guile or warp in him. May he keep so.' There are twenty monosyllables in the former example, twenty-four in the latter (after the word 'flower'). On the other hand, here is Wordsworth, starting with two weighty monosyllables but then going to the other extreme of the language when describing the thick and twisted limbs of a yew-tree: 'Huge trees! And each particular trunk a growth / Of intertwisted fibres serpentine, / Up-coiling and inveterately convolved . . .' The poet writing in English is justified by his subject matter when luxuriating like this in succulent wordiness – this is no lapse of taste or running to excess – but in a sense he is straining at the English language, directing it where it does not really want to go, making it perform well against its natural instinct. As a rule, those who wish to write good English should use short words. The richly inflected Russian language, by contrast, loves to turn long words into even longer ones. The historian, Norman Stone, counsels that when you are learning the language a little alcohol is a great help in 'manouevring those great blocks of polysyllables around the place'. This disparity – rapid, punchy English versus leisurely, massively impressive Russian – means, unfortunately, that the former can never be made to sound convincingly like the latter, except over very short stretches.

This is no reason to despair of translation. When it approximates, it behaves like language itself, which, after all, can paint nothing but shadows of ultimate reality. What is surprising in translation, especially of narrative poetry, is not what is lost, but how much survives. All the acoustics change, which is the greatest loss of all, especially in the case of Pushkin whose instinctive alliterative skills are legendary for all Russians. Nevertheless, some poetic quality will be achieved in a decent verse translation, reminding us always of the original. The story, the characters and all the incidents, by contrast, come through pretty well unscathed, and the narrative tone (particularly significant in *Yevgeny Onegin*, as we shall see) has a good chance also of being preserved. A wide range of humour may hope for successful transmission. Finally, any substantive ideas – ethical questions, philosophical implications, and the like – ought to emerge unsullied. Thus there are rich rewards to be gained from an enterprise which, to some sceptical minds, might appear in advance to be unprofitable. The qualities of this particular translation are outlined in the *Note on the Text*, pp. xxvii–xxviii.

The 'Onegin' Stanza

The happiest decision taken by Alexander Pushkin in the writing of this novel concerns his versification, and particularly the discovery of the 'Onegin' stanza. Although all of Pushkin's previous narrative poetry (and most of it subsequently) was written in flowing paragraphs of verse controlled by a variable rhyme scheme, for *Yevgeny Onegin* he decided to use stanzas. The decision may have been inspired by Byron, who was much admired in Russia, as elsewhere, in 1823. Pushkin is probably half-imitating, half-ridiculing the achievement of *Don Juan*, but in order to do so he has replaced the Englishman's constraining, dully repetitive, *ottava rima* by a marvellously versatile stanza capable of changing shape and renewing itself at the flick of a rhyming switch. Pushkin never describes it as a sonnet, but that is what it is, in essence. The only unsonnet-like quality about the 'Onegin' stanza is that it is written in tetrameters (four-foot lines) instead of the customary pentameters. (Shakespeare himself wrote at least one sonnet (No. 145) using this shorter line). Otherwise, we are presented with the familiar fourteen-line structure which all the European languages have found so accommodating and expressive. It commonly presents two main ideas, of which the second is an extension, culmination or reversal of the first. The Italian sonnet spreads the primary idea over the first eight lines (octave) and its development over the last six (sestet). The English, or Shakespearean, version prefers to let the mind run freely over the first twelve lines (arranged in three quatrains) and then to round things off in a sharp terminal couplet. Pushkin's sonnet-like stanzas cleverly retain for themselves both of these possibilities. The 'Onegin' stanza, while appearing to be a stiff taskmaster, is actually fluid and flexible. A more detailed description of this form is included in *Pushkin and His Critics*, pp. 216–18.

The Mysterious Narrator

Two connected stories are told. Tatyana Larina, an introspective country girl much affected by her reading of sentimental literature, falls in love with Yevgeny Onegin, a bored and arrogant newcomer. She writes to him, but he rejects her offer of love. A few years later the tables are turned. Meeting the new Tatyana, a successful society hostess, Onegin falls in love with her, but it is his turn to be rejected. At the time of their first meeting the second story is recounted, in which Onegin fights a duel with his friend, the young Vladimir Lensky, fiancé of Tatyana's sister, Olga. Lensky is killed.

This fairly simple material is complicated by Pushkin, who has three roles to play in relation to *Yevgeny Onegin*. He is the author, of course; that is straightforward. Less easy to distinguish and assimilate are his two other functions: he is both narrator and participant in his own story. This may not seem important, but in fact it leads us into some subtle difficulties, since the three roles tend to become entangled, losing their distinctiveness. As the author, for instance, Pushkin became so enchanted by his own heroine, Tatyana, that he fell half in love with her. This affection spills over into the telling of the story on more than one occasion when he cannot withhold an exclamation of concern on seeing danger approaching her. When she falls in love, for instance, he calls out in anguish,

My dear Tatyana, in compassion
I weep like you, and for your sake.
For that imperious man of fashion
You seal your fate. By this mistake,
My dear Tatyana, you shall perish . . .
(Three, 15)

These lines clearly indicate the warmth and deep concern experienced by the real poet and/or the fictional narrator, as well as their (or his) inability to intervene in the story to help her, even with advice. On the other hand, his relationship with the hero, Yevgeny Onegin, does extend beyond mere narration to actual involvement in the events recounted. He tells us of their meeting, and what he thought of Onegin:

Now he and I made friends; and greatly
I liked his looks, his special mode
Of oddity, his inclination
Perforce to dreamy meditation,
And cool, sharp intellect . . .
(One, 45)

We learn that Pushkin as narrator was rather overawed by Onegin's stronger, more destructive, personality. We discover that the two of them became very close, to the point of planning a trip abroad together, though this never came about. Thus the teller of the story and one of its leading characters become, like Wordsworth's yew branches, inveterately convolved.

For much of the time the narrator behaves in a fairly conventional manner, simply relating the events as they unfold without significant comment. Even then, however, he gives free rein to his own habit of confiding chattiness; he launches into one agreeable digression after another on a wide range of subjects. On these occasions he is Alexander Pushkin, entertaining the reader with his own ideas rather than directing events or influencing characters in the story. (Incidentally, the digressions are contained and shaped in a disciplined way which sets them apart from the truly garrulous ramblings of Byron, upon which they may well have been originally modelled.)

The obvious conclusion to draw from all of this is that the narrative flow of the novel is deceptive. It is sometimes difficult to determine, or to remember, which particular voice or persona is conducting the commentary at any given time. Above all, one cannot be sure of the narrator's objectivity, since he has admitted his close personal involvement in what is going on. The more he adds to the impression of reality through his wonderfully ingratiating method of narration, the more we must suspect him (as we would any real-life person) of *telling it his way*, subjectively. In most stories you sit back and listen; in this one you go in and out of real life, up and down in sureness of understanding.

There is something particularly Russian in all of this. Literature in that country has been taken so seriously that the distinction between fiction and real life has often been blurred. A good example concerns this very novel. When Pyotr Ilich Tchaikovsky was busy writing his opera based on Pushkin's *Yevgeny Onegin* he too fell in love with the heroine. At that very time he was suddenly approached by an earnest young female admirer, Antonina Milyukova, who wanted him to marry her. Against all his better instincts he accepted her proposal, doing so, as he freely admitted, deliberately in order to avoid acting like Yevgeny Onegin in the novel. Since he was homosexual and she showed marked tendencies towards both nymphomania and insanity, the marriage was a (very short-lived) catastrophe. Ken Russell's film *The Music Lovers* (1970), although accused of titillating sensationalism, may not have been too much of an exaggeration of the ghastliness of the composer's experiences – all brought on because he lost his way in the narrow territory dividing storyland from the real world.

Returning to the novel, we face obvious questions. What is the effect of the narrative mystification, and does it matter? In fact, this is an important issue for several reasons. *Yevgeny Onegin* is a story of bad and foolish behaviour resulting in unhappiness and tragedy. For a full understanding of it we need a clear moral perspective against which to measure the conduct of those involved in the darker incidents. If we are to benefit from their misadventures and come to understand human nature more profoundly, which is one of the purposes of good literature, we need to be able to recognise blame and apportion responsibility. This is difficult to achieve without the certainty of narrative reliability. Specifically, certain rather traditional ways of viewing the characters in this story have grown up over the years. For instance, few people doubt that Tatyana displays tremendous moral fortitude at the end of the novel when declining Onegin's overtures, and most critics agree that Onegin's earlier bad behaviour is mitigated in some way by circumstances or forces beyond his control mostly concerning the age he lives in. In querying these widely accepted judgements ultimately the case stands or falls on its own merits, but it is assisted by our recollection of possible bias on the part of the narrator.

Literary and moral judgement

The story of *Yevgeny Onegin* is told in a manner which makes it impressive, moving and beautiful. No reader will easily forget the imaginative depiction of Onegin's hedonistic, yet unhappy, lifestyle in Chapter One; the many captivating descriptions of town and country life with their delightfully messy bits and pieces; Tatyana's wonderful misadventures, especially her love transports, exquisitely conveyed in a dialogue with her nurse (Ch. Three), and her lurid nightmare (Ch. Five); or Lensky's fatal duel, a *tour de force* of intense poetic realism (Ch. Six). Characters, incidents, scenes and ideas are laid out and developed with the captivating spirit of good poetry. Time after time the sixty-word stanzas (366 of them) strike the imagination with a powerful expressiveness that implies much more than seems possible by such slender means. There is no dissent about the poetic quality of the novel; neither is there disagreement over its elegant structure, sharp sense of observed reality, narrative interest, humour, intelligence or convincing characterisation. These qualities taken together amount to a massive achievement *per se*; given the primitive scene of Russian literature on to which this masterpiece intruded so suddenly, we cannot fail to be impressed by the originality and magnitude of this all-round accomplishment. Like all great works, however, *Yevgeny Onegin* offers much room for discussion; in particular, aspects concerning the motivation and moral responsibility of the characters. Why do the main characters behave as they do, and what are the consequences of their actions?

Much the most interesting issue concerns the personality and behaviour of Yevgeny Onegin himself, a character who seems to have had too easy a time of it with most critics. There has been a tendency to excuse his shortcomings by describing him as a man of strength whose abilities were not only superfluous in the cruel age of Nicholas I, they were actually frustrated, distorted and directed into negative channels by political circumstances. Or by high society and its rigid conventions. Or perhaps because of a kind of spiritual alienation and lassitude (*mal du siècle*) affecting much of Europe at the time. Or even by some malign destiny directing his conduct against his better judgement. The reason behind such charitable attitudes towards his misdoings possibly stems from the author himself, who, as we have seen, had a soft spot for his hero and was also somewhat overawed by him. Certainly Pushkin has succeeded in turning the emphasis in the story away from Lensky's death, which is easily the most significant event, and on to the double failure of the hero/heroine relationship. This ploy has been so successful that it is possible to read summaries of the story which mention only Onegin and Tatyana and omit all mention of Lensky and Olga.

The really significant question is: why does Onegin (effectively) murder Vladimir Lensky? During the duel itself he does everything possible to maximise his own chances of success and minimise those of Lensky. On this occasion there is a real sense of a mature man of the world (in his mid-twenties) using his experience to destroy a youngster (just eighteen). And why does the duel take place at all? Merely because Onegin was in a sulky mood at Tatyana's name-day party, having discovered that the occasion was rather grander than Lensky, in all innocence, had predicted. At this point the operatic version of this story shows two interesting departures from Pushkin's original. The age-gap between the two men has been reduced by Tchaikovsky from about seven to only a couple of years, and the motivation for Onegin's hounding of Lensky has been significantly increased. Onegin overhears guests gossiping about him, which puts him in a bad mood. He is also assisted in his tormenting of the young man by Olga, who emerges as a more positive character in Tchaikovsky's libretto, conniving with Onegin and taunting Lensky with a charge that he is being too possessive and jealous. This is as unjustified as the additional suggestion that he is hot-headed to a point verging on madness. Contrary to received opinion, it has been clearly established that Tchaikovsky, who wrote most of the libretto himself, treated Pushkin's text with great sensitivity, never inventing anything unless he had to do so. This scene is the one exception. It seems likely that the composer could see in the novel so little motivation for Onegin's conduct at the party that he felt obliged to indulge in a little creative adjustment. By doing so he raises, obliquely, the very question which we are trying to answer.

Onegin's persecution of Lensky is *not* motivated by what happens during the celebration; it goes back much further, to the very beginning of their relationship. One explanation of his conduct might be that, in his state of permanent unhappiness despite the many advantages conferred by wealth, education and leisure, he cannot bear to observe anyone so fulfilled and deliriously happy as the young poet on the brink of marriage. If we are to judge by the way he insults Lensky after their very first visit to the Larins', calling his fiancée pretty but stupid, he seems to have set out at the earliest stage to provoke the young man and, perhaps at a deep subconscious level, to destroy him. All of his subsequent behaviour is consistent with this aim, which eventually is achieved with cold determination, Onegin shooting first, with deliberate aim, against an incompetent rival who could never have hit him. There is a good case, at the very least, for looking at this whole pattern of conduct with new objectivity, discounting the broad range of excuses which have so often been paraded to protect the hero. If he emerges as more culpable than was previously thought, perhaps this adjustment of blame and guilt is both justified and overdue.

A similar need for reappraisal arises in the case of Tatyana. She, the best-loved of all Russian heroines (and there are many to choose from), may have been credited with more moral fibre than is justified by her actual circumstances and behaviour at the end of the novel. The received view is that she makes a tremendous gesture of self-abnegation when she turns down Onegin's proposal, but is this really so? Much would suggest otherwise. Following the duel she pays a visit to Onegin's castle, where, reading his books and notes, she starts to see what has escaped her before:

> And as she read, slowly but really
> Tatyana (God be praised, say I!)
> Began to understand more clearly
> The man who'd cost her many a sigh . . .
> (Seven, 24)

This new understanding shows him up as a shadow of a man, a freak, a phantom, an imitation, an empty parody. This awareness of the truth must have stayed with Tatyana only two or three years later, indeed boosted by an equal understanding of the moral outrage which Onegin has committed. He, by the way, is corpse-like and demented by the final chapter, so that pure physical attraction seems improbable. In any case Tatyana is now well-married and unlikely to want to risk her elevated position in society. Her husband is only a dozen years older than her, but Tchaikovsky makes another oblique statement in his libretto. Again sensing a need to enhance weak motivation in the original, he decided to widen the age-gap between Tatyana and her husband to about twenty-three years, in order, it seems, to increase the likelihood of her being tempted into infidelity. The more one reflects on this possibility, in either the novel or the opera, the less likely it seems that Tatyana had great difficulty rejecting Onegin. Rejection is the easy and natural thing to do, as well as being the morally correct solution. The love of which she speaks (Eight, 47) is as implausible as her suggestion, at the start of the same stanza, that she and Onegin had once stood on the very brink of happiness. No commentator has ever suggested that a true love-match between these two characters could have been possible. Tatyana's early misreading of Onegin was based only on her knowledge of heroines in novels (another Russian transgression from fiction into reality, this time within fiction itself). As for Onegin, his own recitation of his undomesticable nature (Four, 12–16) rings only too true. At the end of it all, what Tatyana really loves is, perhaps, the memory of her youth, her books, her house and estate, as well as her old nurse who lies buried there and whom she mentions, rather significantly, just before speaking of happiness and love (Eight, 46).

These two interesting cases illustrate the surprising complexity of *Yevgeny Onegin*, a novel richer in moral, psychological and philosophical overtones than its skimpy story-line alone might suggest. Philosophical is not too strong a word. The poet's many musings on happiness and death, for instance, will provide much to reflect upon for anyone keen enough to collate and contemplate all the references. Not that Pushkin encourages us to do that. He tells his tale with deceptive ease and light-heartedness, as if it is nothing more than superficial entertainment. The fact is that, as with Mozart, this air of insouciance passes a thin veil over what we must recognise as consummate artistic skill, scrupulous organisation and revision of materials, and deep seriousness of purpose. It is in this way that Pushkin sets the standard and example to be followed by the many distinguished Russian writers who were soon to inherit his tradition.

A. D. P. BRIGGS

NOTE ON THE TEXT

The Translation

No fewer than eight full-length English translations of *Yevgeny Onegin* have been made, in not much more than a century. They are all very respectable, despite many a sneer directed at them by the purists. Foremost among these was the formidable Russian writer Vladimir Nabokov, whose own version of the novel, set out in unrhymed though roughly iambic lines, has proved definitive in its accuracy (and a true friend to all post-Nabokov verse-translators), but discouraging in its unEnglish quirkiness. The accompanying commentary, although also full of eccentricities, is a treasure-house of explanatory material.

Oliver Elton's translation, upon which this edition is based, is made from the 1837 edition of the novel (the last to be corrected by the author) and prepared in time for the centenary celebration of Pushkin's birth in 1937. It was described by a contemporary (E. J. Simmons) as possessing sound scholarship, unusual skill and real poetry. More recently John Bayley has expressed the view that 'The several verse translations, notably Oliver Elton's, are all spirited.' It is certainly worth reviving. Perhaps its language sounds a little old-fashioned now, but this may be no bad thing; we do not need too much snappy modernity when harking back to events well over a century old. This point is well illustrated by glancing at a more recent translation by Charles Johnston which, although admirable in many ways, follows a remarkably unPushkinian procedure by removing the capital letters at the start of each line (except where grammar demands them). Presumably intended to encourage fluency in reading the verses, this layout looks like an unfortunate anachronism suggesting the age of Ezra Pound and E. E. Cummings rather than that of Byron. On the other hand, Elton's translation, as well as containing a few inaccuracies, also leans excessively towards the archaic. Consequently, it has been thoroughly revised for this edition. Most of the archaisms have been removed, including convoluted syntax which seemed untrue to the original, and the many uses of the pronouns 'thou' and 'thee'. A large number of feminine rhymes based on participles (e.g. 'Meanwhile a pang her soul is gnawing . . .') have been replaced by more natural speech patterns. A good number of stanzas have been retranslated in their entirety, especially towards the end.

The Names

One of the endearing qualities of the Elton translation is that he gets the important names right. He is the only translator who has taken the correct decision not to translate the names, but to transliterate them. Tatyana, as it happens, presents little difficulty. The only important decision here is to use that spelling rather than 'Tatiana', which may lead, wrongly, to four-syllable pronunciation; Tatyana must be trisyllabic. Onegin is more important and not so easily dealt with. For the record, we should first note that this surname should be pronounced with its first syllable sounding more like an 'a' than an 'o', because the unstressed 'o' in Russian becomes reduced in value. More significant, however, is what happens to his first name. Everybody has taken it for granted that the nearest equivalent English forename, Eugene, will be appropriate. There is a good case for rejecting this, and for retaining the transliterated Russian name Yevgeny, (three syllables rhyming with 'rainy'). The trouble with 'Eugene' is that it strikes the English ear in a manner different from that of 'Yevgeny' on the Russian. To many English-speakers it sounds slightly strange, rather unEnglish. It is uncommon on mainland Britain; most Eugenes are Irish or American. By contrast, 'Yevgeny' sounds middle-of-the-road, thoroughly normal and Russian to a native speaker of that language. We should leave it in Russian, just as we refer to Alyosha Karamazov, Uncle Vanya (not Uncle Johnny), and Yuri Zhivago. Elton deserves credit for being bold enough to do this, though he omits the initial 'Y', which is reinstated here. Russian has two 'e's. The less common one is used mainly for imported words like *elektrichestvo*, meaning 'electricity' and with a first letter not all that different from its English equivalent. The indigenous 'e' is always pronounced 'ye'; hence the word for 'no' being pronounced not 'net' but 'nyet'. It is common for transliterators to simplify by omitting the 'y', but this can lead to mistakes, especially when the 'e' appears in initial position. You will often hear, for instance, the town Yekaterinburg (where the Russian royal family were murdered in 1917) mispronounced as 'Ekaterinburg'; similarly, only people in the know will be able to differentiate between the names Emin and Yevtushenko unless you spell them like that in English, with 'e' or 'ye' as appropriate. For all of these rather complex reasons it seems best to refer to our hero as 'Yevgeny Onegin'. To do so is also to serve the interests of euphony. The name 'Yevgény Onégin' rings with nice poetry deriving from its trisyllabic patterning (two amphibrachic feet, to be precise) and the fact that the two words are virtually a rhyming pair. No formulation based on the name Eugene can come anywhere near this.

YEVGENY ONEGIN

*Dedication**

Pétri de vanité, il avait encore plus de cet espèce d'orgueil qui fait avouer avec la même indifférence les bonnes comme les mauvaises actions, suite d'un sentiment de supériorité, peut-être imaginaire.

(*Tiré d'une lettre particulière*)

A friend's regard is what I care for,
Nor think the haughty world to please;
And fain would I have offered, therefore,
Some pledges worthier than these
Of thy fair soul, thy dreams prophetic
And sacred, to fruition brought,
Thy clear and living vein poetic,
Simplicity, and lofty thought.
Still, take these chapters as I sheave them,
So motley – and be over-kind;
Some simple, some exalted find;
Half-sad, half-mirthful, – so receive them,
These pastimes of a careless mind,
Of wakeful hours, light inspirations,
Of years unripe, of years that wane,
Of cold, keen, reasoned observations,
And signals of a heart in pain.

* To P. A. Pletnev

Chapter One

Precipitate to live, and all too swift to feel.

K. VYAZEMSKY

I

'When Uncle, in good earnest, sickened
(His principles were always high),
My own respect for him was quickened;
This was his happiest thought,' said I.
He was a pattern edifying;
– Yet, heavens! how boring, and how trying.
To tend a patient night and day
And never move a step away!
And then – how low the craft and gross is! –
I must amuse a man half-dead,
Arrange the pillows for his head,
And bring, with a long face, the doses
And sigh, and wonder inwardly,
'When *will* the Devil come for thee?'

2

Such were a young scamp's meditations,
Posting through dusty roads; for he
Was left sole heir to his relations
By Jupiter's supreme decree.
Without more words – my tale this minute
Begins, and has a hero in it.
Friends of Lyudmila and Ruslan,
Let me acquaint you with this man –
Onegin, my good friend, who started
His life on Neva's shores, where you,
Perchance, my reader, were born too,
A shining light. In days departed
I also there would ramble free;
But baneful is the North to me . . .[1]

3

His sire had done good service, living,
Like any gentleman, on debt;
And so, three balls per annum giving,
By ruin was at last beset.
By fate Yevgeny was befriended:
First by a *Madame* he was tended;
Next came a *Monsieur*. But the child,
Though nice, was gay and rather wild;
And therefore, not to overwork him,
Monsieur l'abbé, a needy Gaul,
With pleasant jesting taught him all,
Nor would with moral strictures irk him,
But to the Summer Garden took
The tricksy lad, with mild rebuke.

4

But with Yevgeny once attaining
The age of youth and turbulence,
The age of hope and soft complaining,
They packed the *Monsieur* off; and hence
Onegin was no more imprisoned,
But like a London *dandy* dizened,
And cropt most fashionably, too;
And so, at last the world he knew.
He could express himself completely
In French, and write it, and could dance
Mazurkas with some elegance;
Could bow so easily and neatly.
Enough; the world decides at once
He is a dear, and not a dunce.

5

We Russians get our information
On something – somehow – and so-so;
And thus a brilliant education
Is not so hard, thank heaven! to show.
Onegin (so thought each emphatic
Censor, so rigid and dogmatic),
Though something of a prig, knew much.
On all things talk'd of he could touch
Lightly – not stiffly – , imitating
The visage of the connoisseur
(So fortunate his talents were),
And hold his tongue, through high debating;
Or fiery epigram, meanwhile,
Let fly, and make the ladies smile.

6

'Tis out of fashion now, is Latin;
And yet, in truth, it was no doubt
A language he was rather pat in,
A motto he could puzzle out;
Could prate of Juvenal; none better
Could with a *Vale* end a letter;
Yes, could two lines of Virgil say
With several blunders on the way.
Onegin had no sort of longing
To rummage in the dust of dates
Or chronicles of ancient states;
But to his memory came thronging
Full many a hoary anecdote
From Romulus till now, to quote.

7

It gave him no exalted pleasure
To waste his days in studying sound;
Iambic with trochaic measure
For all our pains, he *would* confound.
Homer, Theocritus abusing,
But often Adam Smith perusing,
He was a deep economist: –
That is, was able to insist
On how a state makes itself wealthy;
On what it lives by; and wherefore
Gold is not needful to its store
If it can keep production healthy.
– His father could not understand,
And mortgaged every inch of land.

8

All the attainments of Yevgeny
Time fails me to enumerate.
But for one science, more than any,
He had a genius past debate.
What gave him – still a child – vexation,
Trouble, and also consolation;
– What all day long engrossed, no less,
His sick and weary idleness; –
Was that fair science Ovid chanted –
The tender passion. Ovid's life
Of riot, brilliancy, and strife
Closed in dull, flat Moldavia; planted
There, as a sufferer ended he,
Afar from home and Italy.

(9)[2] 10

How soon he learned dissimulation
And jealousy, and how to hide
His hopes, and to instil persuasion,
Dissuade, or pine; exhibit pride,
Or humbleness, or sullen bearing,
Or seem attentive – or uncaring!
How taciturn the moody lad!
What flaming eloquence he had!
How careless, in his letters loving!
How self-oblivious he could be,
Breathing of love and constancy!
How quick, how shy, how soft and moving
His eyes – or bold! They could shine clear
Or brim with many a willing tear!

11

How various he seemed – dumbfounding
The innocent with jest and chaff;
His swift despair they thought astounding,
His pleasing flattery made them laugh;
The tender moment he could capture,
Or overcome, by wit and rapture,
The qualms of youthful innocence;
Watch for a heedless kindness – thence
Claim an avowal, by entreating;
Hear the first heart-throb, and pursue
The lover's quest; and quickly, too,
He would secure a secret meeting
And, in some quiet place apart,
Instruct the lady of his heart!

12

Soon he was skilled in agitating
Coquettes, experienced of old;
But when he tried annihilating
His rivals, with what venom cold
He ran them down! and would prepare them
How many a stratagem, to snare them!
You husbands, though, in wedlock blest,
You stayed his friends; he was caressed
By spouses veteran and wily
Of Faublas' school, well trained; or by
Some ancient, with suspicious eye,
– Or by some lordly cuckold, highly
Contented with himself, and life,
And with his dinner, and his wife.

(13, 14) 15

Sometimes, while still abed, they've brought him
A sheaf of notes. – What's here? – By chance
Three houses, really, have besought him
To pass the evening at a dance
Or birthday party. Now, who is it
Our merry man skips off to visit?
And who shall first receive his call?
– No hurry; there is time for all.
Meanwhile, in morning garb, and wearing
A wide-rimmed *bolivar*,[3] he flees
To stroll at large and at his ease,
Unto the boulevard repairing,
Till his *Bréguet's*[4] unsleeping chime
Inform him, it is dinner-time.

16

Dusk falls, and in his sleigh he's posted.
'Hey clear the way,' he calls, 'begone!'
His beaver collar is all frosted
With silvery dust. He hurries on
Straight to *Café Talon*;[5] and therein
He's bound to meet his friend Kaverin;
He enters – vintage juices pop
And corks upon the ceiling plop.
Roast-beef, all sanguinary, greets him;
Truffles (youth's luxury) are seen,
The blossoms of the French cuisine;
And Strasburg pie, unwasting, meets him,
With live and swarming Limburg cheese
And golden pines, to follow these.

17

One beaker more! his thirst compels him
To wash the hot, rich cutlet down;
But now *Bréguet* has struck, and tells him
Of the new ballet in the town.
The theatre's legislator, spiteful,
Inconstant lover of delightful
Actresses – fascinating things! –
Onegin, freeman of the wings,
Leaves. To the playhouse see him sally,
Where all breathe freely; – you may hiss
Cleopatra, Phèdre – and after this
Applaud the capers of the ballet;[6]
Or *call* Moïna. In a word,
Your only aim is to be heard.

18

Fonvizin, satire's lord undaunted,
The friend of freedom, in old time
Shone brightly there, O land enchanted!
Knyazhnìn was there, that witty mime.
There Ozerov was once applauded
With young Semyonova, and lauded
By all the folk, and wrung their tears.
Katenin there amongst his peers
Restored Corneille – high, gifted, glorious.
There won Didelot his wreath of fame,
And Shakhovskoy,[7] the mordant, came
With swarms of comedies uproarious.
There, there behind the scenes, did I
Take shelter, as my youth fled by.

19

And you, my goddesses and graces,
Hear my lament! where are you, where?
Do these new girls, who fill your places,
Displace you? – Nay, are you not there?
And shall I hear again your chorus?
Gaze, as she flies, inspired, before us,
On Russia's own Terpsichore?
– Or will my moody eyes but see
Strange visages, a stage all dreary?
Behold, through disenchanted glass,
An alien world before me pass?
And watch the fun, indifferent, weary,
And say no word, and only yawn,
And brood on matters past and gone?

20

The house has filled; the boxes glisten;
Pit, stalls, are like a seething cup;
The restless galleries clap; – and listen!
The rustling curtain has gone up!
And there, resplendent, in the middle,
Sways, to the magic of the fiddle,
Istomina; her bevy there
Surround that creature, half of air.
First with one foot the floor she brushes,
And on the other slowly twirls,
Then swiftly leaps, and swiftly whirls
Like down by Aeolus puff'd, and rushes,
And coils – uncoils again; – how quick
Her little feet together click!

21

All clap: – Onegin enters, steering
Amid the legs, along the stalls.
His double eyeglass, sidelong peering,
On boxes full of ladies falls;
He knows them not. His glance embraces
Each tier in turn; with dresses, faces,
He's shockingly dissatisfied.
With gentlemen on every side
He next exchanges salutations;
Then scans the stage, all absently,
And turns, and yawns. 'High time,' says he
'Time for all sorts of alterations;
I've stood the ballet long; but oh!
It bores me – even with Didelot.'[8]

22

Snakes, cupids, demons still are leaping
Upon the stage, with wild uproar;
Still are the weary lackeys sleeping,
Wrapt in their mantles, at the door.
Claps, coughs, and hisses are still sounding,
Noses are blown, and feet are pounding;
And still, within doors and without,
The lanterns glitter all about.
The horses, jaded with the leather,
Are kicking still, and frozen through;
The coachmen round the fires beshrew
Their lords, and beat their palms together.
– But exit now Onegin! yes;
For he is driving home – to dress.

23

Can I, with all my artist's passion
Paint that lone room in colours true
Where the prize protégé of Fashion
Is drest – undrest – then drest anew?
– What dainty London keeps retailing
For our caprices never-failing,
And, for our tallow and our wood,
Brings us across the Baltic flood;
– What hungry, tasteful Paris (choosing
A paying traffic) may invent
And for our luxury has sent
As modish, sumptuous, or amusing,
– All these fine things bedecked the scene
Of our young thinker, aged eighteen.

24

Bronze, china, here bestrew the table,
And amber pipes sent from Tsargrad;
Scents in cut crystal vials, able
To make the languid senses glad;
Combs – little files of steel for scraping –
And scissors, straight or bent. For shaping
The nails, or tending teeth, there were
Quite thirty sorts of brushes there.
(Rousseau – I ramble, and admit it –
Could not conceive how pompous Grimm[9]
Durst cleanse the nails in front of *him*,
The golden-tongued, the feather-witted,
But wholly wrong, this once, was he
Who stood for Rights and Liberty.)

25

A man of sense may give attention
Even to the beauty of his nails.
Why fight against the age? Convention
Is the world's tyrant; nought avails.
Yevgeny, jealous censures fearing,
Dressed like Chadayev,[10] now appearing
As what we called a *fop* – was nice
In his apparel, – too precise.
And, facing all his looking-glasses,
Three hours at least he spent, before
He issued from his closet door,
Resembling Venus, when she passes
To join the masquers and assume,
(That giddy goddess) male costume.

26

Your curious gaze I might be turning
On dress – the latest style admired;
Portray, to all the world of learning,
Just how Onegin was attired.
But that were rash, there's no gainsaying;
– 'Tis true, my business is portraying;
Yet still the Russian words we lack
For *gilet*, *pantalon*, and *frac*.
I see – and make you my excuses –
That my poor style would scintillate
Even less, were I to imitate
Such foreign terms, outlandish uses;
– Though once I used to glance upon
Our Academic Lexicon.

27

But that is not our theme – I quit it;
Better to hurry to the ball!
Onegin thither now has flitted
Full tilt, postilion, coach and all.
And now, before the darkened houses
And all along the street that drowses
The pair of carriage lanterns throw
Their rainbow patterns on the snow
And shed a cheery radiance yonder.
That splendid house is spotted bright,
All round, with little cups of light.
Behind the spacious windows wander
Shadows and glancing silhouettes
Of freakish dandies, and coquettes.

28

Our hero to the doors is driven
And darting up the marble stair
Straight past the porter, having given
The final smoothing to his hair,
Enters the hall. The throng has thickened;
The band of its own din is sickened.
In a mazurka spins the crowd;
The people press, the noise is loud,
And the horse-guardsmen's spurs are clashing;
Swift scurry the dear ladies' feet;
After those charming footsteps fleet
How many a fiery glance is flashing!
The fiddles screech. Their clamour drowns
Snide shafts from dames in modish gowns.

29

In days of joyous aspirations,
A ball would leave me reft of wit.
No safer spot for declarations,
For passing letters, none so fit!
Hear, honoured husbands, my proposal:
My service lies at your disposal;
I pray you, mark what I have said;
I like to warn you, well ahead.
And look, you matrons, to your flighty
Daughters, more sharply; keep your glass
Full-focussed on them; else (alas!)
'All's wrong – now save us, God Almighty!'
I write you this because, you know,
I have not sinned – since long ago.

30

Much life, ah me, I squandered sadly
Upon diversions manifold;
Had not my morals suffered badly,
Balls yet could please me, as of old.
I love the youth, I love the madness,
The crush – the glitter – and the gladness –
The ladies' studious finery,
And their small feet. You scarce shall see
Through Russia, shapen to perfection,
Three pairs of feet, in womankind.
But oh, *one* pair, long kept in mind,
Haunts me; in spite of cold dejection,
I still recall them; still, it seems,
They agitate my heart, – in dreams.

31

When – where – or what lone desert threading,
Canst thou forget them, senseless thing?
Where are you, little feet, now treading?
Where crush you now the flowers of spring?
Ah, you have never left your traces
Upon our snowy Northern spaces!
To Eastern languor bred, you much
Adored the sweet, luxurious touch
Of carpets soft, and their allurement.
How long, since I for you forgot
My thirst for fame and praise, once hot,
My native country, my immurement?
The joys of youth have fled indeed
Like those light footsteps on the mead.

32

Lovely is Dian's bosom, charming
Are Flora's cheeks; and yet for me,
Good friends, one thing is more disarming,
– The foot of our Terpsichore.
A presage, to the rash eye gazing,
Of other favours past appraising,
Its beauty, like a symbol, fires
A wayward throng of new desires.
Elvina dear, I love to see it
Beneath the cloth that strews the board;
In spring, upon the meadow-sward;
In winter, on the hearth; or be it
Upon the glassy ballroom floor,
Or rocks of granite, by the shore.

33

Once, by the sea, in stormy weather,
I envied – I remember well –
The blusterous waves which surged together,
When, amorous, at her feet they fell!
And those dear feet aroused my longing
To kiss them, like the billows thronging!
Nay, even in youth, when heart flamed high
And surged within me, ne'er could I
For young Armidas feel such yearning,
Nor ever was I rackt like this
With hope their languid breasts to kiss,
Or lips, or cheeks like roses burning:
No, never did such passion fierce
And gusty rise, my soul to pierce.

34

And one more memory. I am holding
Sometimes, and in my private dreams,
Her happy stirrup, and enfolding
The little foot; and then, it seems,
Again my fancy seethes, excited;
Again her touch the blood has lighted
Within this withered heart of mine;
Once more I love, once more I pine . . .
Enough! my garrulous harp is praising
These haughty creatures far too long;
They are not worthy of my song
Or of the passions they are raising;
And, like those sorceresses' feet,
Their looks, their words, are all deceit.

35

– But what of my Onegin? – Drowsing,
Now bedward from the ball he comes,
While restless Petersburg is rousing
Already, to the roll of drums.
Merchants and hawkers rise from slumber;
Now to their stands the cabmen lumber;
The Okhta milk-girl, see her go,
And hear her crunch the morning snow;
The pleasant sounds of day are waking:
The shutters open; smoke ascends
In columns blue, from chimney-ends;
The German, neat in breed and baking,
All cotton-capped, already has
Raised several times his *vasisdas*.

36

But, with the din of ballrooms jaded,
The child of luxury and whim
Now sleeps, in blessed quiet shaded;
For morning is as night to him.
He wakes past noon: – till morn awaited
By the same life, reiterated,
Motley, monotonously gay,
Each morrow just like yesterday.
– For all his daily round of pleasure
And brilliant conquests, though so free
And in his flowering years, – was he,
Yevgeny, happy in full measure?
Or did he, heedless, healthy, spend
His days in feasting – to no end?

37

Yes – for his heart too soon was frozen;
The noisy world became a bore;
Fair ladies were not long the chosen
Themes that he hourly pondered o'er.
Of playing false, he soon fell weary;
Friends too, and friendship, all were dreary.
He could not be for ever fain
To drench in flagons of champagne
Beefsteak and Strasburg pies; or scatter
Sharp sayings, witticisms make, –
Not when his head was wont to ache.
The rogue was fiery; but no matter,
Dead sick, at last, he was of all,
Of wrangling, sword, and pistol-ball.

38

There is an ailment – and what brought it
Should have been fathomed long before.
Much like the English *spleen* we thought it;
'Tis 'chondria' in Russian lore.
This overcame Onegin, slowly.
Though loth to shoot himself, and wholly
Averse, thank Heaven! to trying, he
Regarded life quite frigidly.
In salons he would come, appearing
Much like Childe Harold, sullen, dark;
No cards, no scandalous remark,
No sighs too bold, no glance endearing
Could ever move the man; indeed
He would see nothing – nothing heed.

(39, 40, 41) 42

You, first and foremost, he deserted,
Quaint dames, who move in circles high;
For in these days, I must assert it,
The need for *ton* makes people sigh.
Bentham or Say may be expounded
By one of them; I've mostly found it
– Their talk – intolerable stuff,
Albeit innocent enough.
Besides, the creatures are so clever,
So past reproach, magnificent,
So packed with pious sentiment,
So circumspect, – and stringent ever;
So reinforced, so anti-male,
They bring the spleen on without fail.[11]

43

You also, ladies young and pretty,
Whom dashing droshkies drive in state
Through the paved streets of our great city
St Petersburg, at hours so late –
Yevgeny dropt you. For employment,
Forsaking riotous enjoyment,
He shut himself indoors, and then
With a great yawn, took up his pen.
He tried to write – was nauseated
By stiff hard work; no word could he
Bring from that pen – could never be
One of that quickly irritated
Guild, upon whom I must not pass
Judgment – I'm one of them, alas!

44

So he, unoccupied as ever,
And weary of an empty head,
Sat down in laudable endeavour
To make his own what others said.
He shelved his books in serviceable
Order; read, read them; all mere babble!
Imposture, wearisome, or mad;
Not one both sense and conscience had.
For all were crampt in various fetters;
Old things were stale; old madness, too,
Was all repeated in the new.
Women he'd dropt – he now dropt letters;
Swathed shelves, their dusty brood, and all,
In taffeta funereal.

45

I, too, had shunned the bustle lately
And tossed aside convention's load;
Now he and I made friends; and greatly
I liked his looks, his special mode
Of oddity, his inclination
Perforce to dreamy meditation,
And cool, sharp intellect. You see,
I was chagrined, and sullen he.
We both knew passions and their working,
And both of life had come to tire;
In both our hearts was quenched the fire;
And still, for both, there lay a-lurking
Our fellows' and blind Fortune's spite,
Just when our days had dawned so bright.

46

He who has lived and thought, despises
Infallibly his fellow-men.
For him who feels, the phantom rises
Of days that come not back again,
And troubles him. Illusions vanisht
And serpent-memories unbanisht
And old remorse, corrode his heart.
– All this to converse must impart
Much relish: I was disconcerted
At first by my Onegin's tongue;
But to his arguments that stung
Became accustomed and converted,
By jests and sallies half malign
And rancorous phrases saturnine.

47

How oft in summer-time – when nightly
The sky above the Neva's shore[12]
Shines so transparently, so brightly,
And Dian's countenance no more
Upon that joyous mirror dances –
We called to memory old romances,
Old loves, of the dead years that were!
Once more, we felt; and free of care
Once more all silently we waited
And blessed wafts of night inhaled;
And like a prisoner unjailed,
Still drowsy, to green woods translated,
So we in dreams away were borne
To youth, and to life's earliest morn.

48

Here, leaning on the granite, waited[13]
Yevgeny, and regretful stood
(Just as the Poet has related
About himself) in pensive mood.
– All quiet! but for sentries ranging,
Their nightly challenge interchanging.
From far Milyonnaya the sound
Of rattling droshkies echoed round.
Upon the slumbering stream before us
The oars of boatmen dipped and swung,
And in our charmèd ears there rung
A distant horn, or gallant chorus.
But sweeter, to beguile the night,
The tune of Tasso's octaves light![14]

49

O, Adriatic waters surging,
And Brenta! I shall see you plain;
With inspiration fresh-emerging
Shall listen to your witching strain.
Apollo's progeny revere it;
On Albion's proud harp I hear it,
Familiar, like the sound of home;
And, steept in languor, I will roam
On gold Italian evenings, lying
In gondola, upon the tide,
A young Venetian by my side
Silent; or, when her tongue is flying,
The lady to my lips can teach
Petrarchan love, Petrarchan speech.

50

High time, high time for me to reckon
On freedom; comes she at my cry?
I wait for weather, and I beckon
The sails, and haunt the sea.[15] – Shall I
Never with storm-fringed waves be warring,
Or travel swift and freely, sharing
The trackless freedom of the sea?
This element displeases me,
This dry dull shore; I must be flying;
For my own skies are African;[16]
And there, mid Southern surge, I can
Bide, over sombre Russia sighing,
– Russia, where once I suffered, where
I loved: my heart is buried there.

51

Onegin would have been delighted
To see with me a foreign clime;
But we were quickly disunited
By fortune, for some length of time.
Just then, his father died. Approaching
Were greedy regiments encroaching
Of creditors, to face. You'll find
There are diversities of mind;
He hated litigation dearly.
And now, contented with his fate,
He made them over his estate.
Perhaps he would not lose severely;
Perhaps he scented, well ahead,
That his old uncle would be dead.

52

And so it was. The steward told him
Quite suddenly, by letter, how
His bedrid uncle would behold him
Gladly, to take farewell. So now,
The sad communication reading,
Our friend, who travelled post, was speeding
Hard to the interview. On chance
Of money – yawning in advance –
He made that careful preparation
(With which my tale began) to lie,
To suffer boredom, and to sigh;
Flew to his village-destination,
But uncle there *laid out* he found,
Ripe for bestowal underground.

53

The servants thronged the court; up started
From every side, to make their call,
Friends, or unfriends, of the departed,
All in full cry for funeral.
So the deceased was buried duly;
The job seemed finished well and truly
By pope and guest who drank and fed,
When off, all solemnly, they sped.
Onegin, once a wastrel sorest,
Loather of order, now must fill
His place as village lord of mill
And soil, of waters and of forest.
His former course of life he had
Exchanged – for something, and was glad.

54

And yet the open country lonely,
The dusky oakwoods, cool and dim,
And quiet, bubbling streamlet, only
For two short days seemed new to him;
And, by the third, lay all unheeded
Copse, field, and hill; they then succeeded
In sending him to sleep; and next,
He was too plainly bored and vext.
And yet in spite of rustication
Away from palace, street, and ball,
And cards, and poetry, and all,
Like a sharp sentinel on station,
Chondria, shadowed, dogged his life;
As does a too devoted wife.

55

To me, the quiet life is native,
The silent country; buried here,
Far sooner flowers the dream creative,
The harp speaks louder and more clear.
My rule is *far niente* – note it;
To harmless leisure all devoted
I range the solitary lake;
On every morrow I awake
To freedom and sweet ease. Not reading
Greatly, I sleep my fill and rest.
Ephemeral fame is not my quest.
When I, in years gone by, was leading
This idle, tranquil life I praise,
Now, were not those my happiest days?

56

Yes, flowers, and love, and country places,
And indolence, you have my heart!
I like to notice that our cases –
Mine and Onegin's – are apart;
So that no readers who are scoffers,
And no stray publisher, who proffers
His laboured web of calumny,
Spying herein some traits of *me*,
May next be ruthlessly reciting
How I, like Byron, bard of pride,
Daub my own portrait glorified;
As though we never could be writing,
In poetry, of other men,
But always paint ourselves again.

57

All poets (apropos) by nature
Incline to amorous reverie;
I dreamed of many a charming creature
Long since; my soul in secrecy
Preserved her image safe; and, later,
Arrived the Muse, to animate her.
So I, light-hearted, of my young
Ideal mountain-maiden sung,[17]
And of the captive ladies lying
Upon the banks of the Salgir.
Your question, friends, I often hear,
'Tell us for whom thy harp is sighing?
Of all these jealous maids who throng,
To which dost consecrate thy song?

58

'Whose gaze hath stirred thy inspiration?
Whose loving-kindness doth repay
The music of thy meditation?
What goddess is thy theme today?'
– No woman, none, my friends, I swear it;
Love's wild distress – I had to bear it;
No consolation has been mine.
Blest he, who can with love combine
The rhymer's fever, and redouble
The poet's sacred frenzy; – so
In Petrarch's footsteps he may go
And pacify his pangs and trouble,
And snatch, in passing, some repute;
Whilst I, in love, was dulled and mute.

59

Love fled; then dawned the Muse, to carry
Light to my spirit's gloom profound.
Now freed, I seek once more to marry
Feeling and thought to witching sound.
I write, with soul no longer pining,
Nor is my heedless pen designing
By marge of stanzas incomplete
The heads of women, or their feet.
No spark flares now, the ash is dying;
No more I weep, though still I smart;
Soon, soon to silence will be flying,
Traceless, the tempest in my heart;
And then will I commence a song
Full five-and-twenty cantos long.

60

Long on my hero's name I brooded,
On how to shape my plot and style;
And now behold, I have concluded
The story's Chapter One, meanwhile.
Severely have I scanned my fictions;
Abound they may in contradictions,
– I care not to correct them; nay,
To censorship my dues will pay,
Give fruits of toil and preparation
For journalists to browse upon.
To Neva's shore now get thee gone,
My youngest, latest-born creation,
And earn for me the wage of fame,
– Clamour, and crooked words, and blame!

Chapter Two

O rus!

HORACE

O Russia!

I

The country nook, that bored Yevgeny,
Was just a thing of pure delight
We should thank Heaven for, as any
Lover of harmless pleasure might.
A hill from all the winds excluded
The master's house; it lay secluded
Above a stream, and far away
Stretcht flower-besprinkled meadows gay
With golden fields of harvest blended.
A village twinkled here and there;
Herds roamed the pastures everywhere;
A huge wild garden, too, extended
Its dense and canopying shades,
A haunt for musing Dryad maids.

2

And here a castle was erected
As castles should be: firmly based,
Quiet, a fabric much respected,
In the old, clever, charming taste.
The rooms were many and high; brocaded
Silks on the parlour walls paraded,
Ancestral portraits also, while
The stoves were shot with many a tile.
Now all had long been antiquated,
I know not rightly why, indeed;
My friend, however, had small need
Of this; nor cared he if he waited
In ancient, or in modish hall;
It mattered not – he yawned in all.

3

In that same room, his habitation,
With housekeeper had ancient laird
Been squabbling for a generation;
Squashed flies, and through the window stared.
All things were plain and serviceable:
Two cupboards – downy sofa – table –
No spot of ink – an oaken floor.
Onegin pulled each cupboard-door:
And one contained a memorandum
Of spendings; one, liqueurs in rows;
There, jars of apple-juice repose.
For books – (the old man never scanned 'em,
He was too busy) – mark the date! –
An almanac of Eighteen-Eight.

4

Alone in his domain, and caring
Merely to pass the time, our friend
Yevgeny first thought of preparing
The ancient order to amend.
Our sage, remote in isolation,
Altered the yoke of old taxation
From toil exacted, for light rent;
And the serfs blessed what fate had sent.
His thrifty neighbour, though, sulked wryly
In his own nook, since he himself
Would suffer horribly – in pelf.
Another smiled upon them, slily;
Then, with one voice, they said they knew
That he was mad – and dangerous, too!

5

At first, they all drove in to greet him;
But, since they mostly found that there
His Don-bred colt was brought to meet him
Round at the hinder entrance-stair,
So he could slip off down a byway,
Hearing their rough carts on the highway, –
Such doings merely could offend;
They ceased to treat him as a friend.
'Our neighbour is a boor, and crazy;
Freemason, too! Red wine, we think,
In glasses, is his only drink.
To kiss a lady's hand, too lazy!
He says plain *yes*, plain *no* withal
Without the *sir*!' So cried they all.

6

Just then, a landowner, a stranger,
Came flying down to his estate,
From neighbours equally in danger
Of the same rigid estimate:
Vladimir Lensky. He his spirit
Did straight from Göttingen inherit;
Handsome and in his prime was he:
Poet, and Kant's own devotee;
And he brought solid fruits of learning
Away from cloudy Germany,
And dreamed when all men should be free.
An oddish soul – yet hotly burning;
Enthusiast in talk; and set
Upon his neck were curls of jet.

7

For him the world had never blighted
With aught to chill him, or degrade;
His soul could still be warmed and lighted
By welcoming friend, or kindly maid;
His heart, so inexperienced, bless him!
That none but hopeful dreams caress him.
The new, bright, noisy world could blind
And capitivate his youthful mind.
Sweet were his visions; he kept under
All doubts that in his heart could rise;
The goal of life was in his eyes
A lure, a riddle, and a wonder.
He vext his head with questionings,
Surmised extraordinary things.

8

Somc soul-mate, he believed, was fated
A fellow-soul in him to find;
And inconsolably it waited
For him from day to day, and pined.
And all his friends – or so he read it –
Would go to gaol to save his credit,
And their strong arm would never fear
To pulverise the slanderer.
The destinies were consecrating . . .[1]

9

Pity, and righteous indignation,
And glory, with its sweets and pains,
And love, pure love, for his salvation,
Were throbbing early in his veins.
Schiller and Goethe had inspired him
And their poetic flame had fired him;
Beneath their heaven, harp in hand,
He wandered over every land.
And he was happy, never shaming
His lofty and artistic strain;
But, proudly singing, would sustain
The loftiest sentiments, acclaiming
The charm of simple dignity
And passionate, virgin reverie.

10

And still his song with love was laden
And love's allegiance, – clear and fair
As musings of an artless maiden
Or a child's dream, or moon that bare
In the calm, empty heaven is lying,
Goddess of secrets and soft sighing.
He sang of parting, and of pain;
Of dim horizons, – and again
Of what? – romance, and roses blowing?
He sang far lands, where on the breast
Of peace, of old he long would rest
While, fountain-like, his tears were flowing;
And how life's flower had blanched unseen;
– This, when he had not turned eighteen.

11

Here, in the wilds, Yevgeny rated
His gifts aright; none other could;
And most of all the feasts he hated
Of households in the neigbourhood.
He shunned their loud confabulation.
So sensible their conversation
About the brandy, and the hay,
Their kennels, and their kin, – but nay,
'Tis not conspicuous for feeling,
Nor for intelligence, nor wit
(Poetic fire is far from it),
Nor yet for skill in social dealing!
'Tis not so clever, but far worse,
When their belovèd wives converse.

12

Lensky was welcome in all quarters,
Rich, handsome, and a bachelor;
And all the dames designed their daughters
(Our country custom this, of yore)
For him – 'quite *half* a Russian, truly!'
He enters – and the talk shifts duly
Aside, upon the weary life
That a man lives without a wife.
Then to the tea-urn in the middle
They call him. Dunya, pouring, hears
The whisper, 'Mark you!', in her ears;
And next she fetches out her fiddle,
And – O, good Lord! – is whining now
'Come to my golden castle, thou! . . .'

13

But no desire for wedlock's fetter,
Be sure, had stirred in Lensky yet.
He longed to be acquainted better
Now with Onegin. They had met;
But each from other more diverse is
Than fire from ice, or prose from verse is,
Or rock from billow. Such, these two.
At first they bored each other, true,
And incompatibly were mated;
But then came liking; then would they
Ride out together every day;
And soon could not be separated.
Thus (I must hasten to confess)
Men become friends – through *idleness*.

14

Such friendships now have wholly vanisht
All men we count as *noughts*, you see,
(Having all prejudices banisht);
We are the *units*, only we.
Napoleon is our ideal;
Feelings are wild, absurd, unreal;
For us a million bipeds are
Merely an instrument of war.
Yevgeny could be tolerated
Better than most, although he knew
Mankind, and chiefly scorned them, too.
But some folk he discriminated
(No rule is quite unqualified);
He honoured feeling – from outside.

15

He smiled at Lensky, and he listened.
The poet's talk, its fire, its thrill,
Eyes that with inspiration glistened,
His brains, his judgments wavering still,
Refresht Onegin, who each moment
Checkt his refrigerating comment
Upon his lips; 'Why mar,' thought he,
'His moment of felicity?
No, that were stupid: on reflection,
A time will come, whate'er I say;
So, let him go, meanwhile, his way,
Believing in the world's perfection.
Let us forgive the fever-heat
Of youth, and youth's delirium sweet.'

16

And oft they fell to disputations
That tempted them to think and brood:
– On pacts of long past generations;
The fruits of science; evil, good;
Old prejudices, still abiding;
The unknown doom the grave is hiding;
Fate, and the haps that life befall;
– They passed their judgment on them all.
The poet, still with theories burning;
Obliviously spouted forth
Fragments of verses from the North;
Yevgeny, lenient, though learning
Little from what he heard, in truth,
Gave all attention to the youth.

17

But still the passions interested
Our hermits most. Onegin, now
By their fierce empire unmolested,
With sighs, that rose he knew not how,
Discussed them, some compassion showing.
And happy is the man who, knowing
Their stir, now leaves them well alone.
But happier he who has not known;
Who cools his love by separation,
His hate with spiteful talk; who ends
By yawning amongst wife and friends,
Unvext by jealous indignation;
Nor, to the tricksy *deuce*, trusts all
His grandsire's honest capital.

18

When to the standard we are flying
Of tranquil reason, and her rule,
And when our passions' flame is dying
And we begin to ridicule
Their wilfulness and all their sallies
And their belated after-rallies,
Then, with a struggle, we are tame;
But sometimes like to hear the same
Wild speech of passion, in a stranger;
It stirs our heartstrings. So, while penned
In his forgotten hut, may lend
An eager ear to tales of danger
Some crippled veteran, – when they're told
By young, moustachioed heroes bold.

19

Hot youth itself is never able
To hide a secret; for relief,
'Tis ever ready with its babble
Of love and hatred, joy and grief.
Onegin, thinking love was ended
For cripples like himself, attended
Gravely; the poet told the whole,
Rejoicing to confess his soul,
His every scruple frankly baring
In perfect trust. Yevgeny knew
His young love-story through and through
Quickly enough, and now was sharing
A tale full-charged with feelings – known
To us long since – our very own!

20

Ah, love like Lensky's! but we know it
No longer, we, in times of late;
And only some insensate poet
Will still love on; for such his fate –
One dream, that nowhere, never fails him;
One wish, that constantly assails him,
And one, too constant, grief that stings!
And not the chill that distance brings,
Nor long-drawn years of separation,
Nor yet the Muse, who steals our time,
Nor beauties of a foreign clime,
Learning, or noisy recreation,
Availed; his soul was still the same,
Warmed by a pure and maiden flame.

21

Charmed while a lad, without a notion
How hearts can suffer, he would gaze
On Olga with a new emotion,
And on her childish sports and ways.
Screened by a guardian oak, he shared them;
Their fathers, friends and neighbours, paired them
And planned the children's wedding-wreath.
There, in her lone retreat, beneath
The humble shelter, overflowing
With charm and innocence for dower,
The parents saw their Olga flower
Just like a hidden lily blowing
Unnoticed, in the thickest grass,
By bees and butterflies that pass.

22

Our poet found that Olga fired him
With youth's first dream of ravishment.
The thought of Olga still inspired him
And drew his pipe's first low lament.
Gone, golden dreams of recreation!
He fell in love with isolation,
And with tranquillity, with night,
With densest woodland, with starlight,
With the moon's lamp in heaven shining;
To whom we oft would dedicate
Our stroll, on misty evenings late,
And weep, to ease our secret pining.
Now, a mere substitute she seems
For our dim, tarnished lantern-gleams.

23

Always so modest, acquiescent,
And cheerful as the morning skies;
Frank as a poet's life: – and pleasant
As lovers' kisses; and with eyes
Of azure like the heavens, and tender;
And smile, and flaxen hair, and slender
Figure, sweet voice, and movements free,
– All this was Olga; you may see,
No doubt, her traits in what romantic
Story you will; I vow to you,
I loved them once myself, 'tis true,
Yet soon they nearly bored me frantic;
Bear, reader, with my taking next
Her elder sister for my text.

24

Her name, Tatyana,[2] be it noted,
Is by our will, and not by chance,
By us for the first time devoted
To usage in a soft romance.
Well, 'tis a pleasant name, and ringing,
Although inevitably bringing
The times of old to memory
Or the maids' attic. And yet we
Must own that little taste has brightened
Our choice of names (and as for verse,
I hold my peace, for there 'tis worse).
Skin-deep, no more, are we 'enlightened';
And what is left us of it all
Is merely – to be finical.

25

Tatyana was her name – so be it;
She had not Olga's pretty face,
So taking, that all men could see it,
Nor her fresh colouring and grace.
She was mute, shy, and melancholy,
Timid as woodland hind; and wholly
A stranger lass she seemed to be
In her own house and family.
And never could her sire, or mother,
Win her caress; she did not care
To join the children's mob, or share
Their sports and gambols like another;
But often by the window lay
And said no word, the livelong day.

26

And Reverie, her playmate daily
From infancy, brought many a dream
That tinted to her eyes more gaily
The country life's too leisured stream.
The needle, her unhardened finger
Knew not; and never would she linger
Bent o'er her frame, with some design
Of silk, to make bare linen fine.
A child betrays our love of ruling:
With her obedient doll will she
Prepare to play propriety
– The world's great law – in jest and fooling;
To dolly, gravely will repeat
The lessons learned at mummy's feet:

27

But Tanya did not care for nursing,
Young as she was, her doll, or choose
With dolly to be found conversing
On fashions, or the town's last news.
All childish pranks were foreign to her;
Rather would tales of horror woo her
And on her spirit lay their spell
When the dark nights of winter fell.
And when the nurse collected for her
Her little friends, she never ran
To play at 'catch-me-if-you-can'
In the big meadow. It would bore her
To hear the ringing mirth, the noise
Of giddy, romping girls and boys.

28

She loved the first anticipations,
Seen from the balcony, of day.
The choral dance of constellations
On the horizon pales away,
And the world's rim grows softly clearer
While zephyrs bring the morning nearer
And the day slowly comes to birth.
In winter-time, when half the earth
Under the realm of night is shrouded,
Longer and longer sleeps the dawn
In sluggard idleness withdrawn,
In presence of a moon beclouded.
Aroused at the same hour of night,
Tatyana rose by candle-light.

29

Romances were her only passion,
And all the world to her; and so
She fell in love, the dupe of fashion,
With Richardson, and with Rousseau.
Quite a good fellow was her father,
Of the last age, belated rather;
He saw no mischief in a book,
Though in one he would never look;
Thought it a toy, and held it lightly,
And cared not what his daughter did
When she a private volume hid
Beneath her pillow, slumbering nightly.
His lady wife was mad upon
The tales of Samuel Richardson.

30

Her Richardson she did not care for,
To read him; no, nor yet because
She judged that Grandison was therefore
A better man than Lovelace was;
But, long ago, a Moscow cousin
Alina, a princess, a dozen
Times had been harping on them both.
And even then, he held her troth,
The spouse to whom she had been plighted
Without her choice, against her will.
While she for one was sighing still
Who heart and mind much more delighted: –
Sergeant of Guards, a buck well known,
A gambler, was this Grandison!

31

Like him, she was herself attiring
Becomingly and in the mode;
– They took her, though, without inquiring
Her will, – in wedlock her bestowed.
And then, to give her grief diversion,
Her canny husband made excursion
Post-haste, unto his country place.
Lord knows how many a stranger's face
Begirt her there! She first lamented,
Writhed, with her husband all but broke;
But then assumed the housewife's yoke,
And habit left her well contented.
Heaven's gift is habit; let us bless
That substitute for happiness![3]

32

Her sorrow none the less persisted,
But yet by habit was beguiled.
One great discovery assisted;
Soon she was wholly reconciled.
Amidst her labours and her leisure
She found the secret, at her pleasure
Steering her husband as she would.
Then all things went on as they should.
She drove about, on business faring;
In winter, salted mushrooms; went,
Shaved peasants' brows,[4] her money spent,
On Saturdays to bath repairing;
And beat the maids (nor cared to seek
Her husband's leave) when in a pique.

33

And tender girls, her albums gracing,
Of old she limned in gory red;
Praskovya's vulgar name replacing,
She drawled 'Polina, ma'am', instead.
She laced her corsets over-tightly;
Our Russian *n* she said, not rightly,
But like the French one, through her nose.
But swiftly all was changed, and those
Stays, album, and 'princess Polina',
And quires of soulful poetry,
Were all forgot. Hereafter she
Would say 'Akulka', not 'Selina';
Her wadded dressing-gown she wore
At last, and night-cap, as before.

34

Her husband gave her warm affection;
With her concerns he would not deal;
He trusted her, without reflection,
And ate and drank in dishabille;
And so his life slid on, quiescent.
Sometimes, at evening, there were present
Some friendly neighbours, not inclined
To stand on forms, and nice, and kind.
Some small regrets, a little laughter
Of sorts, a little scandal – well,
So the time goes. Meanwhile they tell
Olga to make the tea; thereafter
Is supper; and then bedtime's come,
And all the visitors go home.

35

And, in this peaceful life, preserving
The kind of customs, one and all,
And many a Russian pancake serving
In the fat week of carnival,
Twice they devoutly fasted yearly.
Round-swings, round-dances, loved they dearly;
Carols at Yule; at Whitsuntide,
When all the populace gaped wide
Hearing the service, with emotion
They just would let a tear or so
Down on a tuft of lovage flow.
Nor could they breathe without their potion
Of kvass; and every dish was prest,
By rank and order, on the guest.

36

So both grew old, like other mortals;
And then, at last, the grave before
The husband must throw wide its portals;
And now, no marriage crown he wore.
An hour before his dinner dying,
He was bewailed by neighbours sighing,
And faithful wife and children, far
More honestly than most men are.
Plain gentleman was he, good-hearted;
And, where his ashes now were laid,
The monument above him said:
– 'An humble sinner, now departed,
One Dmitri Larin, brigadier,
God's bondsman, tasting peace, lies here.'

37

And Lensky, back again and staying
Amidst his household gods hard by,
Went to that peaceful tombstone, paying
His neighbour's dust a votive sigh.
His heart was deeply, long, affected;
'*Poor Yorick*!' he exclaimed, dejected;
'He bore me in his arms, and I
So often played, in infancy,
With his Ochakov decoration!
He planned that Olga I should wed;
"Could I but see the day! . . ." he said.'
So, full of honest lamentation,
Vladimir, for memorial,
Wrote, on the spot, a madrigal.

38

Here, too, he wept and venerated
His parents' patriarchal dust,
And his sad legend dedicated.
Ah, in life's furrowed fields, we must
Hourly see reapt the generations,
By heaven's secret dispensations.
They rise, they ripen, and they fail,
And others follow on their trail;
And even thus our race, light-minded,
Grows and is troubled, seethes and raves,
And crowds its forbears in their graves.
And our time, ours, will come; we'll find it
Fitting when our grandchildren too
Out of the world crowd me and you!

39

Meanwhile, my friends, drink deep, or rue it,
Of this our life, so fragile; yes,
I am not greatly bounden to it,
I know too well its nothingness.
I shut my eyes to all illusion;
And yet my heart is in confusion
At times, with far-off hopes; and I
Should think it sad to quit and die
And leave no faintest mark in story.
I live, nor write, for praise, be sure;
Yet I would fain, it seems, secure
For my sad fate some share of glory.
One ringing word, befriending me,
Would keep my name in memory,

40

And stir the heartstrings of some stranger.
Perchance some stanza I have penned,
By fate or luck preserved from danger,
May into Lethe not descend.
Perchance, one day, some ignoramus
– A flattering outlook! – at my famous
Portrait may point, and may declare,
'A *poet* – was that fellow there!'
So, take my thanks and gratulations,
Disciple of the peaceful Muse,
Thou who in memory dost choose
To keep my fugitive creations;
Whose hand, in pure goodwill, is led
To pat the old man's laurelled head!

Chapter Three

Elle étoit fille, elle étoit amoureuse.

MALFILÂTRE

I

'Where are you off to? Oh, these poets!'
'Onegin, I must go!' 'Please do.
If there's one thing I'd like to know it's
Just where you keep on driving to.'
'The Larins'' 'Wonderful! Your neighbour.
But isn't that like heavy labour
And don't you find the evenings pall?'
'Of course not.' 'Really, not at all?
I see the scene from where I'm sitting.
Now, first, you will agree with me,
Here's a plain Russian family
Lavishing all care, as is fitting,
On guests – much jam, eternal talk
Of cowsheds, rain and flax in stalk . . .'

2

'Still, I see nothing yet that harms one.'
'The harm, my friend, is just – ennui.'
'I loathe your modish world; what charms one
Is a home circle; there I'm free . . .'
'What now, another pastoral ditty?
Good Lord, dear man, hold hard, have pity!
– Well, must you go, to my regret?
Yet listen: will you never let
Me look upon your Phyllis, newly
The object of your pondering,
Your tears, rhymes, pen, – of everything?
Present me.' 'It's a joke!' 'No, truly.'
'Delighted.' – 'When?' – 'This minute; why,
We shall be welcome, you and I;

3

Let's go.' And off they gallop quickly;
Make their appearance; and they see
Loaded and lavished on them thickly
That old-time hospitality.
The well-known entertainment meets them;
Jam, handed round in saucers, greets them;
And bilberry-decoctions are
On the waxt table, in a jar . . .[1]

4

Quite soon they are again careering
Homeward, now by the shortest way;
Hardly can we help overhearing
Our gallants' conversation. – 'Say,
Onegin, why these yawns? what takes you?'
'My habit, Lensky.' 'Something makes you
More bored than ever.' 'No, not *more*!
But look, the plain is darkening o'er;
Andryushka, hurry, hurry quicker!
This place is stupid. By the way,
Old Larina is nice; she may
Be simple, yes. But ah, that liquor
From bilberries – I fear it will
Do me no good, but make me ill.

5

Now tell me, which one was Tatyana?'
'Why, she who with so sad an air,
So taciturn (just like Svetlana),[2]
Came in, sat near the window there.'
'What, does the younger one allure you?'
'Well?' 'Were *I* poet, I assure you
I'd pick the other. Olga's like
That young Madonna of Vandyke;
Her features I'd call lifeless, even.
Her face is just as round and red
As yonder stupid moon o'erhead
Up in that no less stupid heaven.'
Vladimir answered drily, nor
Upon that journey spoke he more.

6

Meantime, a notable sensation
'Twas for the Larins, one and all,
To see Onegin. Recreation
It gave the neighbour-folk withal:
Guess followed guess; and every moment
Was heard a furtive, whispered comment,
A spiteful judgment, or a scoff.
Tatyana soon they married off;
And some of them had even pleaded,
That marriage had been well in train
And only was delayed again
Since fashionable rings were needed
And Lensky's wedding – why, we know,
That they had settled long ago.

7

Tatyana listened with vexation
To all such gossip; and yet she
With inexpressible elation
Must muse upon it secretly.
She was in love: that thought was grounded
Deep in her heart; her hour had sounded!
So drops a grain in earth; in spring
To life enkindled, quickening.
Long since, her fancy had been burning
In sadness and in languishment,
And craved the fatal aliment.
Long had heart-weariness and yearning
Pent her young bosom; her soul pined
For someone – who was undefined.

8

Now he had come. Her gaze was clearer;
''Tis he!' she told herself at last.
Alas, one image, ever near her
Daily and nightly, overcast
Each fevered dream, and all things told her
Of *him*; dear maid, some spell controlled her!
And wearisome the very sound
Of an endearing speech she found,
And all the sedulous servants, staring.
Sunk in dejection, not a word
Spoken by visitors she heard
She cursed their leisured ways and bearing,
And their arrivals unforeseen,
And thought, 'How long that stay has been!'

9

But now behold with what devotion
She reads each sugary romance
And quaffs the false beguiling potion
Whose lively charms her heart entrance!
Creatures who win their inspiration
By force of happy meditation,
Like Julie's favourite, Wolmar,[3]
Malek-Adhel and De Linar,
And martyred Werther, the defiant,
And Grandison beyond compare,
Who makes *us* slumber in our chair:
– All, for our dreamer soft and pliant,
Assume one vesture in the end
And in Onegin's image blend.

10

A heroine in imagination,
– Julie, Clarissa, or Delphine,
Of some loved author the creation –
She roams the quiet woods unseen,
Alone, the perilous volume bearing;
And pores therein, and finds it sharing
Her visions, and her secret fire,
Fruition of her heart's desire.
She sighs, she whispers, swift to borrow
– By rote – a letter that will do
For her beloved hero too:
Another's joy, another's sorrow!
– Whatso our hero you may call,
He was no Grandison at all.

11

Time was, the fiery author, pitching
His language in the loftiest key,
Showed you his hero, still enriching
Him with each perfect quality;
And this loved object was unfairly
And always harried, and most rarely
Gifted with sentiment, and mind,
And looks of an attractive kind,
And with the purest passion glowing,
Ever in raptures: his one quest,
To sacrifice his interest:
The final chapter always showing
How vice was punished, and the good
Wearing the garland, as it should.

12

Our wits are all befogged at present;
A moral makes us sleepy; nay,
Even in a story, vice is pleasant
And likeable, and wins the day.
The British Muse with any fable
To vex a damsel's dreams is able;
And see, she idolises now
The Vampire with the pensive brow,
Or prowling Melmoth, glum, distressful,
The Corsair, or the Wandering Jew,
Or else Sbogar,[4] mysterious too.
Lord Byron's whim was too successful:
He clothed his self-absorbed despair
With a romantic, weary air.

13

All senseless stuff, my friends; we know it:
And now perhaps, by heaven's decree,
I shall no longer be a poet;
Some other fiend will enter me.
I will scorn Phoebus' frowns, and wholly
Descend to prose, however lowly;
Then some old-fashioned tale shall still
Engross, and cheer, my path downhill.
Not there shall grimly be invented
A villain's secret pangs of soul,
But just a Russian house's whole
Annals shall simply be presented,
With love's alluring visions, and
The antique manners of our land.

14

I'll tell the father's simple greetings,
Or the old uncle's, and their talk;
The trysts of children, and their meetings
By stream or ancient limetree walk;
Sad jealousy, its fierce vexation;
The tears that heal a separation;
Will set them quarrelling anew,
And, in the end, will wed the two.
The words of longing, love, and rapture
And passion, uttered on my knees
To some beloved mistress – these
Words of old days, I will recapture;
My tongue shall learn again at last
The disused language of the past.

15

My dear Tatyana, in compassion
I weep like you, and for your sake.
For that imperious man of fashion
You seal your fate. By this mistake,
My dear Tatyana, you shall perish,
For all the blinding hopes you cherish,
Invoking sombre joys like this,
Eager to know life's sweetest bliss
While drinking of a magic poison.
You are beset by idle dreams.
In every nook a meeting seems
Something to set your hopes and joys on;
In every place you now await
Your tempter, master of your fate.

16

So she, love's quarry, sick and dreary,
Goes down the garden to lament,
And lowers her fixt gaze, too weary
For walking, and too indolent;
When, suddenly, her bosom rises,
A flying flame her cheek surprises;
Breathless, with dazzled eyes, she hears
A noise of thunder in her ears.
Night is at hand; the moon patrolling
Circles the heavenly arch remote,
And through the misty skies comes rolling
The nightingale's sonorous note.
Tatyana, wakeful, and her nurse
There in the quiet gloom converse.

17

'Oh, I am sleepless; nurse, sit near me;
Open a window, or I choke!'
– 'What ails you, Tanya?' – 'Tired! 'twould
  cheer me
If of the good old times we spoke.'
– 'What should we speak of? I was able
Once to remember many a fable
And deed of long ago; I had
Stories of maids, of spirits bad;
But all things now before me darken;
I have forgotten what I knew.
My turn has come, 'tis bad, but true;
And I am stricken now.' 'But – hearken!
Nurse, in the old days, in your youth,
Were you in love? Tell me the truth.'

18

'Stay, child; folk then were never given
To hearing about love. Praise be!
My husband's mother, now in heaven,
Would just have been the death of me.'
– 'But then your marriage, nurse, how came it?'
– 'Why, God's plain will it was to frame it.
Yes, I was in my fourteenth year.
Vanya was younger still, my dear.
For two whole weeks the dame[5] was calling
Upon us, to arrange the troth.
At last, my father blest us both,
And I cried sadly – 'twas appalling;
They wept as they undid my hair,
Took me to church, and sang me there.

19

'To a strange household I departed.
But you've stopped listening. Now, look here . . .'
– 'I am so weary and sore-hearted,
I feel so sick. Oh nurse, my dear,
I'm fit to sob, I'm near to wailing . . .'
– 'My child, my child, you must be ailing.
God save you now and pity you!
Say what you want. What can I do?
I'll sprinkle you with holy water;
You're burning!' – 'Not with illness, no!
Nurse, dear, I am in love – 'tis so!'
– 'Ah, may the Lord be with you, daughter!'
And with frail fingers, as she prayed,
She signed the cross above the maid.

20

'In love' – the murmur was repeated
All sadly, to the nurse. 'My own,
You are not well!' But she entreated,
'In love! Yes, leave me here alone.'
And while they talked, the moon was raying
Her languid lustre down, and playing
Upon Tatyana, pale and fair,
Her tears, her stream of loosened hair,
And on the dame's grey head, well-snooded,
And on her woman's jacket neat
While she, reposing on the seat,
Faced our young heroine; all things brooded
And drowsed as in a tranquil dream,
Under the moon's inspiring beam.

21

But far Tatyana's heart had wandered
And farther, as she watched the moon.
A sudden thought was born; she pondered,
And cried, 'Nurse, leave me; I am soon
For bed; but first, I beg you get me
Paper and pen, and also set me
The table nearer; so, goodbye.'
Alone – all still – the moon shines high!
She, on her elbow leant, inditing,
Dreams of Yevgeny all the while;
Her innocent, unstudied style
Breathes of a maiden's love. The writing
Is done and folded up. But stay:
All this, for *whom*? My Tanya, say!

22

I have known beauties quite unreachable,
As wintry, cold, and pure as ice,
Inscrutable and unbeseechable,
Unbuyable at any price,
Stylish and haughty. 'Tis astounding.
Born virtuous, too – still more confounding!
I own, away from them I fled,
Thinking in horror that I read
Upon their brows the legend hellish,
Abandon hope for ever, you!
To kindle love annoys them, too;
To scare you stiff, is what *they* relish.
You, friends, perhaps have seen before
Such ladies, upon Neva's shore.

23

With tame adorers round them thronging
Some other freakish dames I've known,
Indifferent to sighs, or longing,
Or praises – selfish to the bone.
One thing I marked, amazed me sheerly:
– They, with their bearing, so austerely
Would frighten a shy love, and then
Contrive to lure it back again,
At least by signals of compassion;
At least, the language that they found
Had now and then a softer sound,
Whereon, in the old credulous fashion,
The blind young lover would pursue
His cherished, idle quest anew.

24

Is Tanya worse than these? you blame her
That in her dear simplicity
She knows of no deceit to shame her,
Believing in her dream? that she
Loves, with no thought of artful dealing?
Is swept along, obeys her feeling,
And all too easily confides?
And has some gifts of heaven, besides,
– A fancy, soon tumultuous turning,
A living will, a living wit,
A stubborn headpiece guiding it,
A tender heart, and hotly burning?
And can you no forgiveness find
For all these passions, rash and blind?

25

No flirt's cold-blooded calculation,
No jest, is Tanya's love, but true;
She yields, without one reservation,
To love, as a dear child may do.
She says not, 'Hold him off! so shall you
Of love enhance the market value,
And lure him safer in the net.
Sting first his vanity, and let
Him hope; then rack him beyond measure,
Bewilder him; and then, you see,
You fan the fires of jealousy.
For else, when he has had his pleasure,
Your artful slave is bored, and fain
To choose his hour to snap the chain.'

26

Another problem looms: I'd better,
Indeed I must, beyond dispute,
Translate for you Tatyana's letter,
To save my country's good repute.
In Russian she was poorly grounded;
She never read our journals; found it
Too great a toil to speak her mind
In her own language; was inclined,
Therefore, to write in French. Despairing
Again I ask you, what to do?
Our ladies have not, hitherto,
Their loves in Russian been declaring.
Our lordly tongue cannot compose
As yet, epistolary prose.

27

The ladies – yes, they would constrain them
To read in Russian; but I think
Of that with horror; and to feign them
Handling *The Well-Disposed*,[6] I shrink.
Now, I appeal to every poet:
When those dear objects (well you know it)
To whom in private, many times,
You all have penned so many rhymes,
To whom your heart is consecrated,
– So feebly, with such heavy toil,
Learned Russian – was it not to spoil
And, oh, so sweetly mutilate it,
That on their lips that alien tongue,
Transformed, like native Russian rung?

28

Heaven save me, when I leave, from meeting
Upon the stairs, or at the ball,
Some capped academician's greeting,
Or student in a yellow shawl!
I hate that Russian talk should err not
In grammar, just as I prefer not
The rosiest lips that never smile.
But, to my grief, perhaps meanwhile
The beauties of our generation
(Because the papers so implore)
Will teach us grammar and its lore
And will put rhymes in circulation.
But what care I? for I shall be
Still faithful to antiquity.

29

Their faulty speech, their careless babble,
Their mispronunciations bold,
Still in my bosom will be able
To stir a tremor, as of old.
I can't feel penitent; at present
I find their gallicisms pleasant,
Like sins of youth that we rehearse,
Or Bogdanovich[7] making verse.
Enough: my own young beauty's letter
Is now my business. Did I give
My promise? Nay, but as I live,
I think to take it back were better.
I know that Parny's tender style
Has been outmoded, this long while.

30

Wert thou still here, who singest[8] sweetly
Of *Banquets*, and of woes that pine,
I should disturb thee, indiscreetly,
And beg of thee, dear friend of mine: –
'Translate my passion-ridden maiden's
Words to thine own enchanting cadence,
For foreign are those words.' But thou,
Where art thou? come, for I do now
Salute thee, all my rights conveying . . .
But no: beneath those Finnish skies,
Where cheerless rocks around him rise,
With heart disused to praises, straying
In solitary banishment,
His spirit hears not my lament.

31

Tatyana's letter never tires me
To read; and when I read it now,
I hold it sacred; it inspires me
With a sad, private pang, I vow.
Who taught her in soft words to render
Her love, so heedless and so tender?
Such touching nonsense – to impart
All the wild language of her heart,
So baneful in its fascination.
I know not – a pale copy give,
No more – the picture does not live –
A feeble, incomplete translation;
Just so a schoolgirl's finger may,
All timidly, *Der Freischütz* play . . .

'That I am writing you this letter
Will tell you all; and you are free
Now to despise me; and how better,
I wonder, could you punish me?
But you, if you can promise ever
One drop of pity for my fate,
Will not have left me desolate.

'I wished at first, believe me, never
To say a word, and then my shame
Had been unknown and of small blame,
Could I have hoped, but once a week
Here in our village, when you came,
To see you, and to hear you speak,
And pass a single word of greeting,
Think of you only, night and day,
And wait – until another meeting.
You are not sociable, they say;
The solitude, the country, bore you.
We are not smart in any way;
But always had a welcome for you.

'Why came you? why to *us?* alone,
In this forgotten hamlet hidden,
I never should have known you, known
This bitterness of pangs unbidden.
And these emotions would have slept,
My soul its quiet ignorance kept:
One day I might have come to find,
Who knows? a husband to my mind,
And been a true wife – to another,
A pious, honourable mother.

'"Another"! . . . I would ne'er have given
To living man, this heart of mine!
This was the will of highest heaven,
This was appointed: – I am thine!
All my past life assurance gave
That we should meet – as though to bind me;
God sent you here, I know, to find me,
And you shall guard me to my grave . . .

'Often you came in visions to me,
You were my friend, though unseen still,
Your tones reverberated through me,
Your wondrous glances sapped my will
Some time since . . . No, I was not dreaming.
You came upon me, all-redeeming,
I knew you then, took fire, stood numb
And my heart told me, 'He has come!'

'Is it not true? In deepest stillness
I heard you, for you spoke to me
Whilst I was giving charity
Or praying to allay the illness
Which kept my soul in agony.
Are you, today, not he who came
And seared the limpid darkness, nearing
My very pillow? The selfsame
Beloved vision reappearing?

'Are you a guardian angel to me,
Or crafty tempter to undo me?
Resolve my doubts and my confusion;
It may be, this is all for nought
And an untutored soul's illusion,
And fate quite otherwise has wrought . . .

So be it, but henceforth I yield me,
And all my fate, into your hand;
I weep, and here before you stand,
Entreating only that you shield me.

'Conceive it: I am here, and lonely;
None understands me; and if only
My reason were not faint and weak!
But I am lost, unless I speak.
I wait on you. One look will quicken
The hopes that in my bosom dwell,
And one reproach deserved too well
Will snap the spell which holds me stricken.

'No more of this; I dread to read it;
Yet, though I sink with fear and shame,
Your honour keeps me safe; I plead it,
And to it boldly trust my name.'

32

Tatyana moaning sits, or sighing,
And grasps the quivering written sheet;
The rosy wafer shrivels, drying
Upon her tongue at fever-heat;
Upon her shoulder she is propping
Her head; the thin light robe is dropping
Down from the charming shoulder. – See,
The radiance of the moon will be
Gone presently; the mists are breaking,
The valley clears; and on the stream
Yonder there steals a silver gleam.
Morning! The shepherd's horn is waking
The village; now the world's astir;
But Tanya – all is one to her.

33

The day has dawned; she never knows it;
She sits, head bowed upon her breast;
The letter waits; she will not close it;
Her graven seal is not imprest.
But see, the door is softly swinging;
Grizzled Filipyevna is bringing
Her mistress' tea upon a tray.
'Get up, my child, 'tis time, 'tis day!
– Why, beauty, you have finished dressing!
My little early bird, last night
You nearly made me die of fright!
But you are well, by Heaven's blessing!
Of the night's sadness, not a trace;
Now you are blooming, poppy-face!'

34

'Please listen, nurse, to my petition.'
'What is your bidding? Tell me what.'
'You must not think . . . there's no suspicion . . .
You know . . . Oh, please. Refuse me not!'
'My love, by Heaven – hear me swear it . . .'
'This note, then – let your grandson bear it
Quite privately, to On . . . or, well,
To *him*, our neighbour. Strictly tell
The lad to take it, never saying
One word; nor must he name me, no!'
'But where, my love, is it to go?
My senses, nowadays, go straying.
So many neighbours are in call,
I cannot even count them all.'

35

'But nurse, how slow you are to take me!'
'Well, Tanya, I am old, dear heart,
I'm old and dull; my wits forsake me;
There was a time when I was smart;
The master would just say, "I want it" . . .'
'But what of that, good nurse? I grant it;
I do not need your wits; the need
Is that the letter should make speed
Unto Onegin.' 'Well, so be it;
But be not cross, my heart's delight;
You know, I am not over-bright.
You're turning pale again, I see it!'
'Nurse, truly, all is well with me;
But send your grandson, instantly.'

36

No answer yet; one day has fleeted.
Another comes; still nothing; why?
Full drest at dawn, she waits to meet it,
Pale, ghostlike; when will he reply?
– But here is Olga's swain admiring;
And now the hostess is inquiring –
'But tell me, where's your friend? Somehow
He has forgot us all, I vow.'
Tatyana flushed and shivered, vainly.
'He promised he would come today,'
Said Lensky to the dame, 'He may
Be kept by correspondence, plainly.'
Tanya looked down, as though she heard
Reproach and malice in that word.

37

Upon the table sputtered, gleaming,
The samovar, as darkness fell;
Light wreaths of vapour up were steaming
To heat the china teapot well.
And next the fragrant tea was going
Into the cups, and darkly flowing,
By Olga's ministry poured out;
The page-lad took the cream about;
But Tanya by the window lingers;
Breathes on the icy glass; and she
(I love her!) lost in reverie
Is tracing, with her charming fingers,
Upon the misted pane, *E.O.*:
A sacred monogram, we know.

38

Her spirits droop. What is the matter?
Her tired eyes overbrim with tears.
– Her blood runs cold: a sudden clatter,
Horses outside, a trot! She hears
Yevgeny! With an *oh!*, and springing
Light as a shadow, Tanya, flinging
Into the hall, down garden-stairs,
Flies on, flies on, and never dares
To look behind, but swiftly hurries
Round bridge, parterre, and mead, and brake,
And alley leading to the lake,
Bursts through the shrubs and lilacs, scurries
Through flower-beds to the brook. Dead beat
And panting, now upon the seat

39

She drops . . . 'Yevgeny here, great heaven!
He's here – what can be in his mind?'
Her heart, by many a torment riven,
A hope still nurses, dim and blind.
'He'll follow' – Burning, trembling, fearing.
She waits – his step she is not hearing!
(The maids, among the bushy rows,
Were gathering berries in the close,
Singing in chorus. They were bidden
Sing, for good cause: to see that they
Should not on master's berries prey
With roguish lips, while safely hidden,
But be kept busy with their song;
Such tricks to country wits belong.)

Girls' Song

Maidens, O you pretty things,
Company of loving ones,
Maidens, go ye frolicking,
Darlings, in your revelry!
Strike ye up your roundelay,
Roundelay and ritual;
See ye lure the lad to us
Where we circle round about!

When we lure the lad to us,
When we see him distantly,
Darlings, let us scatter then
And with cherries pelt at him,
Cherries, and with raspberries,
And with currants, ruddy ones!
Never come to listen at
Roundelays of ritual,
Never come to spy upon
This our maiden merriment!

40

Tatyana heard them as they chanted,
But, heedless of the voices shrill,
Waited impatiently, and wanted
Her throbbing bosom to be still
And her flushed cheek to blaze no longer.
And yet her heart beat ever stronger;
The blaze upon her cheek remained
Fierier than ever, brighter stained.
Thus some poor butterfly will quiver
And flutter with its irised wing,
Caught by a schoolboy frolicking;
Thus, in the winter corn, will shiver
A leveret, when far off he spies
The covert where the marksman lies.

41

But Tanya, with one sigh, departed
At last; and rising from her seat
She went; but presently she started
Into the alley – there to meet
Yevgeny! there he faced her, seeming
Like some grim ghost; his eyes were gleaming;
And she, as though a fiery flare
Scorcht her all over, halted there.
Today, dear friends, I am not equal
(For I must take a walk, perforce,
And breathe after so long discourse)
To telling you, at length, the sequel
Of that unlookt-for meeting. – Nay,
I'll finish it, somehow, some day.

Chapter Four

La morale est dans la nature des choses.

NECKER

7[1]

The less we love her, when we woo her,
The more we please a woman's heart,
And are the surer to undo her
And snare her with beguiling art.
Men once extolled cold-blooded raking
As the true science of love-making:
Your own trump everywhere you blew,
And took your loveless pleasure too.
Such grave and serious recreation
Beseemed old monkeys, of those days
(Our grandsires') that have won such praise:
But now the musty reputation
Of all the Lovelaces is dead,
With gorgeous wigs, or shoe-heels red.

8

Who is not sick of canting – saying,
In other phrase, things said before?
Of solemn efforts at conveying
Assurance – when we all were sure?
Hearing the old objections ever;
Dispelling prejudice – though never
A vestige of it had there been
In any damsel turned thirteen!
Who is not sick of execrations,
Of threats and prayers, affected fears,
Gossip, deceptions, rings, and tears,
Six-folioed communications,
And aunts and mothers watching you?
– The husband's onerous friendship, too!

9

Even such Yevgeny's meditations!
The victim from his youth, of old,
Of his tempestuous aberrations,
Ridden by passions uncontrolled,
His pampered way of life had harmed him.
For one thing, for a time, had charmed him.
But the next disenchanted him.
Then, slowly tired of lust and whim,
And tired of flighty, cheap successes,
He feels, amid the hush, or din,
A ceaseless murmur, deep within,
And, with a laugh, his yawn suppresses.
So, for eight years he killed the time,
Wasting the blossom of his prime.

10

Though love of ladies fair now swayed him
No more, he dangled – glad enough
To breathe again, when they betrayed him,
And soon consoled for each rebuff.
Quite without rapture, he pursued them,
And then without a pang, eschewed them;
Almost forgot their love, their spite.
– Thus some indifferent guest, at night
To play a game of *whist* arriving,
Sits down; and when the rubber ends,
He promptly now departs, descends,
And homeward, to his nap, is driving.
Next morn, himself he does not know
Where, that same evening, he will go.

11

But keenly was he touched and shaken,
When Tanya's missive he perused.
Her girlish dreams had power to waken
A swarm of troublous thoughts confused.
That charming Tanya, he reflected,
Had seemed so pallid, so dejected –
And deeply now immersed was he
In sweet, in blameless reverie . . .
Though heats of old familiar nature
Perhaps possessed him for a while,
He was not minded to beguile
An innocent and trusting creature.
– But now unto the garden let
Us fly, where he and Tanya met.

12

Two minutes pass, and yet they speak not.
Then, drawing near, Onegin said:
"'Twas you that wrote to me – and seek not
To disavow it. I have read
Your trustful spirit's free confession;
And this outpouring, this expression
Of guileless love's sincerity,
So lovable, has stirred in me
The pulses of long-silenced feeling.
I would not offer praise; but now
Will, in repayment, all avow
In words as artless and revealing.
So, hear my shrift; myself, and it,
To your fair judgment I submit.

13

'Now, had the life I chose confined me
To the domestic round; and should
Some pleasing fortune have designed me
For marriage, and for fatherhood;
Had I, one instant, been enchanted
By pictures of a home: – I grant it,
I would have sought for none beside
Yourself – 'tis true! – to be my bride.
I speak no tinselled verse, no fiction;
'Tis true! – as my first dream, my own,
I would have chosen you alone
To share the days of my affliction,
As pledge of all things fair and bright,
And won – what happiness I might!

14

‘I was not made for joy; my spirit
Is alien to that blissful lot;
All the perfections you inherit
Are useless; I deserve them not.
For us – and take my word’s assurance –
Marriage were torment past endurance.
However strong my love may be,
Custom will quench it, speedily.
Next, will come tears; but all your weeping
Will never touch my heart to ruth,
– Will simply madden it, in truth.
What roses, then, is Hymen keeping
In store for us? bethink you well!
Perhaps for long? ah, who can tell?

15

‘What home on earth is sadder-fated
Than where the wife must make her moan,
To an unworthy husband mated,
All day, each evening, left alone?
Where her bored man, while duly rating
Her virtues, still goes execrating
His lot? In scowling silence, he
Rages with frigid jealousy.
Even such am I! – and were you seeking
This in that letter, where is seen
Your pure and fiery spirit speaking,
Your heart so frank, your wit so keen?
Can such a doom have been assigned
To you, by destinies unkind?

16

'Past years, old dreams, no resurrection
Can find, nor I my soul renew.
I give you brotherly affection,
And, maybe, something tenderer too.
So, be not angered; lend me hearing:
– A young girl's visions, often veering,
Lightly from dream to dream may range;
Just as a sapling tree will change,
New leafage every springtime bearing;
For such is heaven's apparent will.
You, too, will love again; but still . . .
Learn self-control! Will all be sharing
My comprehension, my belief?
No: inexperience leads to grief.'

17

Thus spoke Yevgeny, sermonizing.
Meantime Tatyana, though she heard,
Was blinded by her tears arising,
Scarce breathed, and answered not a word.
He gave his arm; and, silent wholly,
She leaned upon it, melancholy;
'Mechanically', as they say,
Home, round the garden, went her way,
Her little head in languor bending.
Though seen together, no one thought
Of disapproving them in aught.
Our country manners unpretending
Their happy right of freedom claim
While haughty Moscow does the same.

18

You, reader, will agree precisely
With me: to Tanya, in her woe,
Our friend comported himself nicely.
He had been known, before, to show
That noble, upright disposition,
Though people's malice and suspicion
To him were wholly merciless.
Onegin's foes – his friends no less –
(There may be little difference, say you?)
Abused him up and down. All men
On earth must have their foes; but then,
Lord, save us from our friends, I pray you!
– Those friends! those friendships, above all
I have good reason to recall.

19

Yes, well? – this idle rumination
So gloomy, now may sleep, for me.
One parenthetic observation: –
There is no scurvy calumny
Hatcht in a loft; no liar's babble,
Encouraged by the social rabble;
No imbecile remark or hint,
No epigram of vulgar mint,
But your good friend, who smiles so gently,
Will, in a ring of decent folk,
Ten times (all wrong) repeat the joke
All without spite, all innocently;
Yet stay, through all, your partisan,
He loves, as only kinsmen can!

20

Ahem! most honoured reader, let me
Ask, – are your family all well?
And might it please you to permit me
This opportunity to tell
The accurate signification
Of the words *family, relation*?
– With love and kindness we are bound
To treat relations; with profound
Respectfulness; to go to see them
At Yule – our custom national;
Or, through the post, to greet them all.
Thus, for the twelvemonth, you will free them
From giving you one thought; and so,
Long years God grant them, here below!

21

Yet lovely women's love, so tender,
Gives brighter hopes than friends or kin;
Your claims on love you'll not surrender
Through all life's tempests, with their din.
No doubt: and yet the whirl of fashion,
The wilfulness of woman's passion,
The tide – of what the world thinks right . . .
Ah, that dear sex is feathery-light!
And then a virtuous dame, moreover,
Utmost consideration vows
To the opinion of her spouse;
Thus our true mistress from her lover
Is in a moment swept away:
With love, the Devil makes great play!

22

Who can be loved, and who be trusted?
Who will keep faith with us? – not one.
Who has each act, each word adjusted
To ours, in sweet compliance? – none.
Who sows no slanders, to offend us,
Or cares to cherish us, or tend us?
Who, in our faults, no harm can see?
Who, never once, can cause ennui?
– No, honoured reader! I advise you,
Just love – yourself! No more in vain
Be wasting all your toil and pain
Or chase a phantom-shape that flies you;
Believe me, you will never find
An object worthier, or more kind.

23

There are no prizes for divining
The sequel of that interview:
How that young soul continued pining,
Thirsting for love, and wretched too,
And frantic. Nay, still more her passion
Is one of hopeless desolation,
And fills poor Tanya's fevered head.
For slumber now forsakes her bed . . .
Her health is gone, her smiles are shrouded;
Life's bloom and sweetness, maiden peace,
Are but a hollow sound, and cease;
Dear Tanya's youth is darkly clouded.
Thus shadowing storms enwrap the morn
While day is struggling to be born.

24

Alas, she withers, turning whiter;
Her flame is quencht – and mute is she!
Nothing can interest, delight her,
Or rouse her soul from lethargy.
The neighbours wag their heads, look serious,
And pass the whispered word mysterious,
'High time to marry her, high time!'
– Enough; for now, in haste, my rhyme
Must liven your imagination
With scenes of love and happiness.
My friends, compassion and distress
Constrain me, not my inclination;
So pardon me, if ali my love
For my dear Tanya I would prove.

25

Lensky, each hour more subjugated
By Olga, youthful, fair and good,
With all his soul capitulated
To that delicious servitude.
They are inseparable, – whether
They sit within her room together
At dusk, or to the gardens fare,
Clasp hands, and take the morning air.
And then? – by love enraptured, greatly
Confused and shamefaced, – for a while,
Emboldened by his Olga's smile,
He ventures shyly, delicately,
To dally with a loosened tress,
Or kiss the fringes of her dress.

26

Sometimes to Olga, to delight her,
He reads a moral, sage romance;
(A better knowledge has the writer
Of Nature, than Chateaubriand's!)
Yet some few pages of pure fable
And empty stuff – which still is able
To harm a maiden's heart, no doubt –
Vladimir, blushingly, leaves out.
Or, from the world themselves secluding,
The pair, above the chessboard bent,
With elbows on the table leant,
Are seated, and profoundly brooding.
He, his attention far withdrawn,
Takes – his own castle, with a pawn.

27

When he rides home, at home, intently
He thinks upon his Olga still;
And with her features diligently
Loose leaves of album he will fill.
Views, shrines to Venus consecrated,
Tombstones, are there delineated;
A dove, upon a lyre aloft,
In ink, or colours light and soft.
One page for souvenirs! below it,
Where many another name is signed,
A tender versicle you find,
Mute record of the dreaming poet.
A passing thought leaves a strong trace,
Which all the years cannot efface.

28

You surely will have seen a blotted
Girl's album, in some one-horse town,
By her dear friends all soiled and spotted
From start to finish, up and down.
Herein, with words all spelt at pleasure,
Time-honoured lines, quite void of measure;
They stick, too short, – too lengthy, too –
To prove that friendship can be true.
On the first page you could be reading
'*Qu' écrirez-vous sur ces tablettes?*'
Subscribed with '*t.à.v., Annette.*'
And then, down to the last proceeding:
'*If you have a more loving friend*
Let him write after this. The End.'

29

And there, assuredly, shall meet you
Two hearts – a torch – and flowers in bloom;
And there, believe me, vows shall greet you
Of love, true-hearted to the tomb;
There too some poet-captain, jibing,
A villainous verse has been subscribing.
I too, my friends, am happy, quite,
In such an album to indite;
My heart assures me, doubt I dare not,
That this, my fervent, foolish stuff
Will earn a friendly glance enough,
– Not spiteful smiles – from folk who care not
To ask, all gravely – do I show
Some wit in all my stuff, or no?

30

But you, odd volumes! ever finding
From shelves of libraries your way;
You albums in your splendid binding,
That vex the rhymesters of the day;
Books by Tolstoy[2] once decorated,
By his swift magic brush created,
Or Baratynsky's pen.[3] – I call
On heaven – may lightning scorch you all!
And is some brilliant dame conferring
On me her book, in quarto page?
Why then, I shake, am swept with rage,
And deep within my soul is stirring
A biting epigram; but still,
Go, make them madrigals, at will!

31

No madrigals is Lensky wreathing
In dear young Olga's album, where
His pen of truest love is breathing;
No frosty, glittering smartness there!
For all that he had heard or noted
Of Olga, is to her devoted;
His floods of elegiac verse
Do but the living truth rehearse.
Thus does your passionate heart impel you,
Inspired Yazykov,[4] when your muse
Sings someone's charms (though God knows whose),
And your choice elegies can tell you
At moments, of your own hard fate,
And all its history relate.

32

But silence! Hark! a critic urges
Us all, severely, to fling by
That miserable wreath of dirges;
And to our rhymesters hear him cry
(Our brethren): 'Now, stop all this soaking
In tears, and your eternal croaking
And moaning about *days of yore*;
Chant other themes, or chant no more!'
– Too true: 'tis thy command unerring
To chant of bugle, mask, and knife,
And our dead thoughts to bring to life,
That scattered treasure disinterring.
Friends, am I right? – 'Quite wrong! So, then,
You must write odes – odes, gentlemen,

33

The ode[5] established, as men writ it
In puissant days of long ago'.
– What, only festal odes permitted?
Stop, friend, it matters not; you know
That saying of the bard satiric;
Now, are a poet's artful lyric
And 'meaning strange'[6] as hard for thee
To bear as our sick rhymesters be?
– 'Nay, but the elegy is hollow;
Its purpose woeful, empty, vain;
The ode can boast a lofty strain,
A noble purpose'. Here might follow
For us whole centuries of dispute.
I cannot quarrel; I am mute.

34

Vladimir, vowed to fame and freedom,
Would, in the turmoil of his mind,
(Except that Olga would not read 'em!)
Himself have many an ode designed.
Has ever a tearful bard recited
To her, in whom his soul delighted,
His compositions? We're assured
That such is life's supreme reward!
Ay, when his dreams he readeth to her,
Lovely, beloved, besung, admired,
And – pleasantly – a little tired,
How blest is then the modest wooer!
Blest he – although, perhaps, her thought
May be quite otherwise distraught.

35

The only person I am choosing
For my attempts at tuneful verse
And all my fruits of lonely musing
Is my old friend, my ancient nurse.
No, once the weary meal concluded,
Where some stray neighbour has intruded,
Abruptly then his skirts I twitch,
Breathe tragic speeches in some niche;[7]
Or else (and here I am not jesting)
Weary of rhyming, full of ache,
I ramble out along my lake
And scare the wild ducks from their nesting:
They, when my dulcet lines they hear,
Take flight from shore, and disappear.

37

What of Onegin? – Friends, I owe you
A prayer for patience, by the way. –
I shall describe him closely; show you
How he employed the livelong day:
Lived hermit-wise; was up and doing
At seven in summer, soon pursuing
The path to where beneath the crest
The river flowed; went lightly drest,
And soon that Hellespont was swimming
Like him who sang Gulnare the fair;[8]
Drank off his coffee then and there,
Some miserable journal skimming;
Then, got him clothed . . .[9]

(38) 39

Walks, reading; slumbers deep; and flowing
Waters that gurgle; woodland shade;
At times, a fresh young kiss bestowing
Upon some fair-skinned, dark-eyed maid;
A steed that's docile, though he prances;
A dinner, served to suit one's fancies;
A flask of vintage, clear and good;
Tranquillity, and solitude –
Thus lived his saintly life Yevgeny,
And so became its devotee
Insensibly; nor knew how many
Fine summer days he passed, carefree,
At ease, forgetting city haunts,
And friends, and tiresome festive jaunts.

40

Now, this our Northern summer season
Gleams, and is gone – a travesty
Of Southern winters; for some reason
We will not own it, no, not we!
Too soon, with daylight ever sparer
And blinks of sunlight ever rarer,
We feel the tang that autumn brings.
The woods, with mournful murmurings,
Are stript of secrecy and shadow;
And the wild geese, with shrill parade,
Make for the South, in cavalcade;
The low mist settles on the meadow.
A weary time we must await;
November's knocking at the gate!

41

The dawn comes all in mist, and coldly;
No sound of work – the fields are dumb;
And out upon the highway boldly
The wolf and famisht she-wolf come.
The horse that passes knows him, snuffing,
And snorts; the weary traveller, puffing,
Pelts up the hill. At break of day
No herdsman now can drive away
His cattle from the shed; or calling
At noontide with his horn, can bring
Them round to muster in a ring.
The maid[10] spins in her cottage, drawling
Her song; the matchwood crackles bright,
Good company for wintry night!

42

Behold, the fields are silvered thickly;
The earth is crackling where it froze;
(Reader, the rhyme – and take it quickly –
That you are waiting for, is – *rose*!)
The ice-clad waters flash and glimmer;
No stylish, scoured parquet is trimmer;
The youngsters in a joyous crowd
Score deep the ice; the skates ring loud;
The ponderous, red-toed goose, designing
Upon the river's breast to swim,
Just ventures on the icy brim,
Then slips, and tumbles; whirling, shining.
Gaily the year's first snowflakes pour
In starry showers upon the shore.

43

In these far wilds, this season dreary,
What shall one do? Go walking? – Why,
Just now, the country can but weary;
Its naked sameness jades the eye.
– A gallop on the grim steppe, say you?
But see your steed do not betray you!
The ice will catch his blunted shoe,
And he may founder – so may you.
– Well, under your lone roof sit reading;
Pradt,[11] Walter Scott, are just the men.
No? Turn to your account book, then,
Or chafe, or drink; and so proceeding,
Spend the long evening, and next day.
Thus winter nicely slips away.

44

All idly – and Childe Harold making
His model – will Onegin brood:
He sits in icy baths half-waking,
Then stays at home in solitude,
All day, in his account-books dipping;
Or, with blunt cue himself equipping,
From early morn Yevgeny falls
To dummy billiards, with two balls.
The country evening now is nearing;
The cue's forgot, the game is played;
The table by the hearth is laid.
Yevgeny waits; and now appearing
Is Lensky's troika, with three roans.
– Look sharp, and see the table groans!

45

That blessed wine, produced by Moët
Or Widow Clicquot, in a trice
Was brought to table for the poet,
Chilled, in the bottle, off the ice.
Like Hippocrene it gleams and flickers;
The way it foams and plays and bickers
(Like – choose your own similitude!)
Charmed me; in days of old I would
My last, poor, smallest coin go spending
(Do you remember, friends?) on fizz.
That flow of magic liquor is
The source of follies never ending,
Of jests and verses in a spate,
Of joyful dreams, and gay debate!

46

But, with its riotous foam, I find it
Soon plays my stomach false; and so
At present I am greatly minded
To stick to sensible Bordeaux;
And for Aï[12] still less am fitted:
Aï is like a feather-witted
Mistress, all sparkle, sprightliness,
Caprice, and whim – and emptiness . . .
But thou, Bordeaux, art like a steady
Friend, in our griefs, our evil days;
A comrade everywhere, always,
To render us fair service ready,
Or quiet hours with us to spend.
And so long live Bordeaux, our friend!

47

The fire is dead, with just a shining
Gold film of ashes on the coals;
All but invisible, and twining
Upward, a wisp of vapour rolls.
Warm airs are from the fireplace breathing,
Pipe-smoke goes up the chimney wreathing;
Upon the board the beaker bright
Still sputters, and the mists of night
Are on us . . . How I love the season
When friends may chatter as they will,
And friends once more the wine-cup fill!
They call that hour, for some strange reason,
Between the wolf and dog. Now we
Will hear our friends, in colloquy: –

48

'What of our neighbour ladies, say you?
Tatyana, and the sprightly one,
Your Olga?' – 'Fill me up, I pray you,
One half-glass more – there, friend, have done!
They all are well, they send their duty.
– Ah, Olga's shoulders! still their beauty
Increases! such a bosom, too!
And – what a soul! . . . One day, with you,
Or you'll offend them – I must call there.
Tell me, I put it to you now,
(You've only looked in twice, I vow)
Why, you scarce show your nose at all there?
Dolt that I am . . . see here! and know
You're askt, this very week, to go.'

49

'I?' – 'Yes, a nameday celebration,
Tatyana's, comes next Saturday.
I bring dear Olga's invitation,
Her mother's, too; you must obey
That summons; come!' – 'A mob will be there?
What raggle-taggle shall we see there?'
– 'Who will be there? no soul will be,
I'm sure, save Tanya's family.
Let's go; I ask it as a favour;
You will?' – 'All right.' – 'You're very good!'
And he to *her*, his neighbour, would
Empty his glass; a pledge he gave her;
And next began, in lover's vein,
To talk of Olga once again.

50

Lensky is joyous; fixt and dated
The happy day, three weeks from this:
Day of the raptures long awaited,
The lover's coronal of bliss,
The secret nuptial bed. Nor dreamt he,
Even for a moment, of those empty
Cold fits of yawning, or what pain
And worries come in Hymen's train.
To us – we're Hymen's foes, I own it –
The life domestic only means
Rows of exhausting, boring scenes,
Much as La Fontaine's tales have shown it.[13]
To such a life was, I'll be sworn,
My poor, warm-hearted Lensky born.

51

For he was loved (he liked this fiction)
And happy. Blest an hundredfold
The man of faith who, with conviction,
Rejects pure reason as too cold,
Who rests, in blissful stupour sunken,
Like a reposing traveller drunken,
Or (prettier words) a butterfly
Who sucks the springtime flowers dry.
But wretched he who knows no dizziness,
The all-predicting realist
Who can't stand words, which turn and twist
In all their meanings and their busyness.
Life must have chilled his heart, it seems,
Who cannot lose himself in dreams.

Chapter Five

Oh, thou my Svetlana, experience not these dreadful dreams!

ZHUKOVSKY

I

That year the autumn was belated,
The weather held so long; and still
The world awaited winter, waited
For January to come; until,
On the third night, snow fell. Awaking
Early, Tatyana saw it making
The courtyard and the rooftree white,
And fence and flower-bed; saw the light
Ice-tracery on the panes, the cover
Of silver on the trees; the court
Gay with the magpies and their sport.
The hills, now softly covered over,
Sparkled with winter's carpeting.
White, sharp, and clear was everything.

2

Winter! The peasant's spirit dances;
Again he journeys in his sleigh;
Sniffing the snow, his mare advances
At shambling trot, as best she may.
Past them a bold *kibitka* scurries,
Ploughing the furrows up in flurries;
In sheepskin coat and sash of red,
The driver perches at its head.
Here is a houseboy, bright and breezy,
Transformed into his sledge's horse,
His pup the passenger. Of course,
The young rip's finger-tips are freezing.
It's funny – and it hurts. Alas,
Mama waves warnings through the glass.

3

But such a picture, as I sketch it,
Will, you may tell me, not attract;
''Tis all *mean* nature, wholly wretched,
With nothing exquisite, in fact'.
– Another bard, inspired divinely,[1]
Warmed to his work, and painted finely
Our earliest snows, in sumptuous style,
– All tints of pleasure that beguile
Our winters. Aye, he can allure you
With fiery verse, when he portrays
Secret excursions in the sleighs.
Just now I mean not, I assure you,
To vie with him – or you, whose verse[2]
Doth of the Finnish maid rehearse.

4

Tatyana, knowing not the reason
– For she was Russian to the core –
Adored our Russian winter season
In all its beauty, cold and hoar:
The sunny rime, the frosty morning,
The sledges, and the tardy dawning
When the snows gleam with rosy hue;
The misty Christmas evenings, too:
For all the house kept solemnizing
Those evenings, in the ancient style;
And all the serving-maids, the while,
Of the young ladies were surmising
And yearly promised each one, plain,
A soldier-husband, and campaign.

5

Tatyana trusted all traditions
Come down from simple folk of old;
All the cards said, all dreams and visions,
And whatsoe'er the moon foretold.
By tokens she was agitated;
All things she saw prognosticated
Something mysterious; oft her breast
Was by presentiments opprest.
If puss, upon the stove reposing,
Purred, washed her face with mincing paw,
'Twas a sure sign, Tatyana saw,
Of visitors; and when, disclosing
Her twofold horn, the moon on high
Rode newly in the leftward sky,

6

Then Tanya was all pale and shaking;
And did perchance a meteor flee
O'er the dark heavens, and fall, and breaking
Scatter to nought, then hastily
Would Tanya, flustered and excited,
Before that star had yet alighted,
Whisper the wish her heart concealed.
And if a hare, amid the field,
Should streak across her path like lightning,
Or if a monk attired in black
Should meet her on the way, – alack!
Distracted by a sign so frightening,
Full of misgivings and of fear,
She knew calamity was near.

7

Yet, even while her fears abounded,
A secret pleasure she must own;
For so hath Nature us compounded,
Nature, to contradictions prone.
Yule was at hand, – and such enjoyment!
Guesswork is flighty youth's employment:
Youth has no cause for sorrowing;
For life lies far ahead, a thing
Distant and bright, past all conceiving:
While spectacled old age must peer
And guess, although the grave is near
And all is lost beyond retrieving.
What then? With lispings infantile
Hope still attends it, to beguile.

8

And curiously Tanya gazes
Upon the wax that melts and sinks.
The pattern, with its marvellous mazes,
Announces marvels, so she thinks.
The rings come out, in proper order,
From the dish brimming to the border.
She draws a ring; she hums a rhyme,
A ditty[3] of the antique time:
Riches are there for every peasant:
He shovels silver with his spade;
The man we sing to, he is made
In wealth and fame. But sad, unpleasant,
The burden tells of something lost;
The maidens love the *tomcat* most.[4]

9

A night of frost; no cloud in heaven;
The magic starry chorus flows,
So calm, harmonious and even . . .
Into the courtyard Tanya goes,
Her dress low-cut. She moves, directing
Her mirror at the moon, reflecting
– Only the mournful moon, alas!
Shimmering in the sombre glass.
– Hush! The snow crackles. Someone's coming!
She tiptoes to him, as on wings,
And her low voice more softly rings
Than airs upon a reed-pipe humming:
'*What is your name?*' he looks upon
The maid, and answers, '*Agathon.*'[5]

10

Directed by her nurse, the lady
Would tell her fortunes in the night,
And in the bath-house bade make ready
A table laid for two aright,
All quietly. And yet Tatyana
Was scared; and, thinking of Svetlana,[6]
I'm scared. So we must let things be.
Her spells are not for you and me.
Her silken girdle soon untying,
Disrobed, she lies upon the bed,
Whilst Lel[7] is hovering overhead.
Her maiden mirror, though, is lying
Beneath the downy pillow deep.
All quiet! Tanya is asleep.

11

She dreams a dream, a wondrous vision . . .
She is walking through a snowy glade,
A melancholy intuition
Of sadness and beglooming shade.
In front, amid the snowdrifts roaring,
A gray and gloomy flood is pouring.
Unfettered now by winter's hand
It whirls and foams along the strand.
Across the torrent laid, united
By icicles, are two thin stakes,
– A bridge of death that thrills and quakes;
And here, bewildered and affrighted,
Tatyana halts, before the hiss
And uproar of that dread abyss.

12

And at that plaguy, sundering river
Tatyana can but chafe and chide;
And no one is in sight, to give her
A hand to reach the further side;
When, suddenly, the snowdrift surges!
– Who, who is this that now emerges?
A shaggy, a prodigious bear!
And Tanya screams; he bellows there,
A needle-pointed paw extending
To help her. Gathering all her strength,
She leans upon him; now at length
Her timid footsteps she is bending
Across the stream, with hands that shake.
She's over – Bruin in her wake.

13

To look behind, her courage fails her;
With quickened pace she tries in vain
To slip the hairy brute, who trails her
Like an attendant in her train
And lurches on and growls, past bearing.
Before them is a pinewood, wearing
Its sullen beauty, motionless,
Laden with tufts of snow, that press
The boughs to earth. The stars in heaven
Gleam through the birch and aspen crests
And leafless limes; and now there rests
On bush and steep, by tempest driven,
The snow; and it is piled and tost
So deeply, that the track is lost.

14

She gains the wood, the bear soon follows,
Up to her knees in crumbling snow;
Now suddenly a long branch collars
Her neck, now with a rasping blow
Plucks her gold earrings; now the little
Wet slippers, where the snow is brittle,
Clog her dear feet; now lets she fall
Her kerchief, has no time at all
To lift it. Terrified, and hearing
The pad of Bruin at her heels,
With hands all quivering, she feels
Ashamed to lift her skirts. Careering
She flees; he follows, hard upon;
She flees no more; her strength is gone.

15

She drops upon the snow, defenceless,
And nimbly Bruin seizes her,
And she, submissive now and senseless,
Borne onward, cannot breathe or stir.
With her down forest paths he rushes;
Soon a mean hovel through the bushes
Appears, all buried deep and bound
With desert waste of snowdrift round.
One window there is brightly glowing,
And the hut rings with cries and yells.
'*Here*,' saith the bear, '*my gossip dwells:
Come, warm thee here awhile*.' And going
Straight in the passage, through the door,
He sets her on the threshold floor.

16

There she comes to, and falls a-thinking,
And gazes; vanisht is the beast!
Within are shouts and glasses clinking,
As though at some huge funeral feast.
No rhyme is here, nor reason! Creeping
And through a crevice softly peeping,
What sees our Tanya now? ah, what?
There, round a table, monsters squat!
One dog-nosed creature horns is wearing;
One has a head like Chanticleer;
There sits a witch, goat-bearded; here
A skeleton, prim and proud of bearing;
A short-tailed dwarf; and here, again,
A thing that is half-cat, half-crane.

17

But see, more awful, more surprising!
A crayfish on a spider ride;
A skull, above a goose-neck rising
Red-nightcapped, twists from side to side;
And here a windmill dances, clapping
Its sails, and squatting, clattering, flapping.
Barks, whistlings, banging, song, guffaw,
Voices of folk, and hoofs that paw!
But what is Tanya's meditation
When, plain among the guests, is *he*,
The man she loves, yet fears to see,
The hero of our strange narration,
Onegin! Seated there, askance
Upon the door he casts a glance.

18

He drinks – all drink, and howl thereafter;
He makes a sign; all fuss and hum;
He mocks; and all explode in laughter;
He frowns – and all the crowd is mum.
He is the master there, no error!
And Tanya loses half her terror,
And now in curiosity
Opens the door a thought, to see . . .
And lo, a sudden blast comes dashing
And quenches all the candle-lights;
Confusion takes that horde of sprites;
Onegin's eyes with wrath are flashing;
All rise; he rises with a roar
Up from the board, and seeks the door.

19

Then, panic-stricken, in her hurry
Tatyana struggles to take flight;
But she is powerless; in her flurry
She writhes, and tries to shriek outright;
In vain! Yevgeny slams and closes
The door, and that fair maid exposes
Unto the hellish phantoms' gaze.
A wild and violent cry they raise;
And all those eyes, probosces crooked
And tufted tails and tongues that drip
With blood, and each moustachioed lip,
Horns, hoofs, tusks, bony fingers hookèd,
All point at Tanya: one and all
'*Mine! She is mine!*' – '*No, mine!*' they bawl.

20

'*No mine!*' Yevgeny answers grimly;
And, presto! all the gang are flown.
There in the frosty darkness, dimly,
He and the girl abide alone.
And softly then Yevgeny sways her[8]
Into a corner, and he lays her
Down on a tottering bench, and stoops;
His head upon her shoulder droops.
Then, while a sudden light is flaring,
Comes Olga; Lensky follows nigh;
Onegin waves an arm on high
And rolls his eyeballs, wildly glaring,
Those guests unbidden to upbraid,
While, all but lifeless, lies the maid.

21

The jangle swells – Yevgeny quickly
Grips a long knife – and straight he fells
Lensky – the awful shadows thickly
Cluster – insufferable yells
Resound – and all the hut is shaken –
And Tanya, horror-struck, awakens . . .
She looks about her; it is day
There in her room; a morning ray
Red on the frosted pane is dancing;
And rosier than our northern light
At dawn, and like a swallow's flight,
Comes Olga, through the door advancing.
'Now then,' says she, 'tell me, my love,
Who is it you've been dreaming of?'

22

But she, her sister never heeding,
And lying, book in hand, in bed,
Leaf after leaf turned over, reading,
But not a syllable she said.
That volume held – no revelations,
No poet's sweet imaginations,
No deep wise truth, no pictured scene;
But neither Virgil nor Racine,
Scott, Seneca, or Byron ever,
– No, nor a lady's fashion-sheet,
Caused an engrossment so complete!
Friends, 'twas Martin Zadeck,[9] so clever.
Arch-sage of the Chaldeans, who
Reads and divines your dreams for you.

23

A wandering hawker once had brought it
To their retreat, that work profound;
And Tanya, in the end, had bought it;
Three roubles and a half she found
The price to which the man consented;
An odd *Malvina*[10] he presented
As well; but took (besides the cash)
A sheaf of fables – market trash;
A grammar; epics (two) on Peter;[11]
A Marmontel – just volume three.
And the Zadeck was soon to be
Her favourite. Zadeck would greet her
With solace in all woes; she kept
His volume by her, when she slept.

24

Her dream – she cannot comprehend it –
Perturbs Tatyana; and what fate
By that dread vision is portended
She fain would now investigate.
She glances through the *Contents*; here is
A perfect alphabetic series:
Bear – *bridge* – *fir* – *gloom* – and *hedgehog*; next,
Raven – *storm* – *snowstorm* – *wood* . . . the text
Goes on . . . But Martin's book is failing
To solve the doubts that vex her still;
And yet that dream, of omen ill,
Forebodes much matter for bewailing.
And so, for some few days, her mood
Is one of deep disquietude.

25

But lo, from out the eastern valleys,
While the sun follows at her call,
Dawn, with her purple finger,[12] sallies
For that blithe nameday festival.
From early morn the guests arriving
Throng in the Larins' house; and driving
Thither whole neighbour households are
In sledge or carriage, gig or car.
Commotion in the hall, and bustle,
And, in the parlour, strangers meet;
Pugs yap; young girls with kisses greet;
While, by the door, are noise and jostle,
Guffaws, feet scraping, curtseys deep,
While nurses shrill, and children weep.

26

And Pustyakov, with fatness swelling,
Also his portly spouse, we see;
Gvozdin, a landlord all excelling,
Who owns a beggared peasantry;
Those grey Skotinins, who surprise us
With offspring of all ages, sizes,
From two, to thirty at the top;
And Petushkov, the district fop;
My own first cousin too, Buyanov,[13]
With downy face, and peak on cap
(A man well-known to you, mayhap);
The councillor (retired) one Flyanov,
Old ponderous gossip, knave and loon,
Glutton, and grafter, and buffoon.

27

And Panfil Kharlikov then duly
Drove up, with family; Triquet,
A goggled, red-wigged Monsieur, newly
Come from Tambov, a wit; today
(True Frenchman) in his pocket bringing
Couplets for Tanya, made for singing,
Réveillez-vous, belle endormie!
Well known to every child. – You see,
These lines were printed among musty
Old songs in almanacs, and they,
By that sagacious bard, Triquet,
Were brought to light from limbo dusty,
But substituting for Niná
New words: *La belle Tatiyaná.*

28

Lo, from the nearest suburb bowling,
The Captain, leaving his command,
And all the county dames consoling,
The spinsters' idol, is at hand!
Hey, what a new sensation for us!
The regimental band and chorus!
The Colonel sent them, who but he?
It means – a ball! and happy we!
See how they skip for joy, the wenches . . . [14]
But now the meal is served; and so,
In pairs, arms linkt, to dine they go.
The girls, round Tanya, crowd the benches;
The men throng, posted opposite;
All cross themselves, and buzz, and sit.

29

Husht for a moment is the tattle,
And folk are munching. All around
Plates, knives, forks, *et cetera*, rattle;
The glasses jingle and resound.
With gusto – for they do not lack it –
The guests begin to raise their racket,
While no one listens as they shriek
And shout and wrangle, laugh and squeak.
The doors fly wide for Lensky, drifting
In with Onegin suddenly.
'Great Heaven, at last!' is Madame's cry.
The guests all crush together, shifting
Forks, knives, and stools, and call the pair,
And get them seated – ay, but where?

30

– Seated, with Tanya fairly facing!
Pale as the morning moon she stays,
Shocked like a doe whom hounds are chasing,
Keeping her overclouded gaze
Still lowered; burning wildly, seething
With passion, sick with stifled breathing.
The greetings Tanya never hears
From the two friends; and now her tears,
Poor child, are like to fall; and nearly
She faints, and drops. And yet her will
And inner strength of reason still
Prevail at last. Two words she merely
Can murmur, through her teeth, at best;
Then sits at table, with the rest.

31

But nerves and tragic revelations
And girls that weep and faint away
Had tried, of old, Yevgeny's patience;
Familiar inflictions they!
And our odd fellow, wroth at lighting
On that prodigious feast, and sighting
Poor Tanya, languorous and seized
With tremors, dropt his eyes, displeased,
And sulkt and scowled in indignation,
And swore he would to fury wake
Lensky, and signal vengeance take.
Exulting in anticipation,
He started sketching, inwardly,
Burlesques of all the company.

32

And others, too, could well have noted
Tanya's dismay; but every eye
And all attention was devoted
To judging of a fat, rich pie
(Which was too salt, and we regret it).
They bring Caucasian wine, and set it
In tar-rimmed bottle, as is meet,
After the roast, before the sweet;
Then rows of glasses long and slender;
Like your trim waist, Zizi,[15] they seem,
O crystal of my soul, the theme
Of my verse innocent and tender,
The phial of love which charmingly,
Time was, intoxicated me.

33

The bottle pops; the wine can sputter
Freely, the soaking cork away.
Now, long upon the rack to utter
His lines, with solemn pose Triquet
Is up; all wait till he has spoken,
Observing silence deep, unbroken;
Then, holding out a leaflet, he
To Tanya turns (half-dead is she!),
And strikes up, tuneless. Acclamation
And plaudits hail him. She of course
Must curtsey to the host, perforce.
He, first to drink in salutation,
Modest for all his greatness, stands,
And lays his couplet in her hands.

34

Then Tanya thanked them all, for many
A happy wish and compliment.
But, when his turn arrived, Yevgeny,
Seeing her face, so tired and spent,
And her confusion, so appealing,
Now found himself new pity feeling,
And made his bow, without a word;
But somehow, in his glance there stirred
A wondrous touch of kindness. – Whether
All genuinely moved was he,
Or jested, in pure gallantry,
Impulse – goodwill – or both together,
That glance could only kindness show,
And Tanya's heart it left aglow.

35

The chairs scrape back, and with much shoving
Into the parlour streams the crowd,
Stirred like a beehive honey-loving,
Swarming afield and buzzing loud.
Now, with that festal dinner mellow,
Each neighbour wheezes to his fellow;
Dames by the fireplace sit in a ring,
Girls are in corners whispering.
Green tables are at last unfolded.
Boston and omber, as of yore,
Call stalwart players to the fore
And whist, still favoured. Now behold it –
This monolithic dynasty,
These sons and daughters of ennui!

36

Eight lengthy rubbers terminated,
The champions of whist have now
Eight times their places alternated;
And tea is served, – It's fine, I vow,
To measure out my day by dining –
Tea – supper, thus the hours defining,
We country folk the moment know
Unworried – for our stomachs go
Right, like a watch. (I take occasion
To note that in my lines I treat
Of banquets, sundry things to eat,
And corks, with no less iteration
Than thine, O godlike Homer, lord
By thirty centuries adored!)

(37, 38[16]) 39

The tea is served; the girls, decorous,
Just touch their plates; beyond the door
Swiftly bassoon and flute sonorous
Ring out, on the long ballroom floor.
Cheered by the thunderous music sounding,
Now doth the Paris of surrounding
Townships (forsaking tea with rum),
Young Petushkov, to Olga come;
To Tanya, Lensky. Kharlikova,
A damsel now of years mature,
Tambov's own poet will secure;
Buyanov whirls off Pustyakova;
They stream and muster in the hall;
Now, in full splendour, shines the ball.

40

When I began my tale, I meant it
To have (see sheet the first, for plan)
A ball at Petersburg, presented
Quite in the manner of Alban;[17]
But, into idle daydreams falling,
Soon I was busy with recalling
The feet of ladies whom I knew;
And on the slender tracks of you,
O little feet, I strayed completely.
High time I should become, in truth,
Sager than in my fickle youth,
– Reform, in style and doings, meetly;
And this new sheet, my fifth, must I
From all digressions purify.

41

The waltz is whirling now and spinning
In its insane monotony,
– Like youth, when life is just beginning;
Pair after pair goes flashing by.
And now, his hour of vengeance nearing,
Onegin in his sleeve is sneering;
He goes to Olga – circles fast
With her, round all the guests – at last
Gives her a chair – makes conversation
On one thing and another – then,
Two minutes later starts again
With her, still waltzing. Consternation
Is universal, blank surprise;
Nay, Lensky cannot trust his eyes.

42

Then the mazurka rang, sonorous.
Unto its thundering peal, of yore,
The whole vast ballroom rockt in chorus,
The heelstrokes shook the waxen floor,
And window-frames all quivered, griding.
Not so, these days! Now we go sliding
On varnished boards, – as ladies do;
And yet, in town and village, you
May find that the mazurka duly
Its old, primeval beauties keeps.
Heeltaps – moustachioes – little leaps
Remain, unchanged by our unruly
Bad tyrant, Fashion, – who is still
Our modern Russians' chronic ill.

(43) 44

My cousin, then – he's somewhat heady[18] –
Buyanov, to our hero led
Tanya, with Olga. All too ready,
Onegin off with Olga sped.
He takes her, gliding negligently;
Leans down to her; and whispers gently
Some homage, cheap and commonplace,
Pressing her hand. And Olga's face
Wears livelier and redder blushes,
Self-pleased. My poet all has seen,
And, now beside himself with spleen
And jealous indignation, flushes;
Through the mazurka waits, to call
For one cotillion after all.

45

'She cannot.' – Cannot? God in heaven!
But what is this? and what hears he?
– That Olga has her promise given
Unto Onegin? So, could she . . .
This child coquetting, feather-witted,
Who scarce her swaddling-bands has quitted?
So young, and yet so versed in wile!
So young, so practised to beguile!
Our Lensky, stricken past all bearing,
Damns women's tricks; he will not stay,
Calls for his horse, and leaps away.
For one thing only is he caring: –
Two pistols, and two bullets, straight
And swiftly shall decide his fate.

Chapter Six

Là sotto giorni nubilosi i brevi
Nasce una gente a cui l'morir non dole.

PETRARCH

I

And now, no sign of Lensky seeing,
Onegin, still by Olga's side,
Was plunged in thought, from boredom fleeing
And with his vengeance satisfied.
And Olga yawned, like him; unresting,
Her eyes for Lensky still were questing,
And that cotillion could but seem
Endless – a leaden, wearying dream.
– 'Tis ended! all to sup are speeding.
Beds for the night are made, and all
The guests are shifted from the hall,
Far as the servants' quarters, needing
Quiet and sleep; and to his own
Lodging Onegin goes, alone.

2

All settles. In the parlour this is
The snoring, ponderous Pustyakov
Beside his no less ponderous missus;
Gvozdin, Buyanov, Petushkov,
And Flyanov (seedy) are reclining
On chairs, where they have just been dining;
Triquet lies on the floor, at rest
In his old night-cap and his vest.
The rooms of Olga and Tatyana
Hold all the girls in sleep's embrace.
Sole, by the window, sad, her face
Full in the radiance of Diana,
Poor Tanya tries to sleep, in vain,
And gazes on the darkened plain.

3

He, unexpectedly appearing,
The spark of kindness in his eye,
And then, the strangeness of his bearing
To Olga: – all have inwardly
Pierced to her soul; she is unable
To fathom him: inexplicable!
Sick, jealous fears perturb her breast,
As though an icy hand comprest
Her heart; as though beneath her lying
Were some tumultuous, dark abyss . . .
Says Tanya, 'I shall die of this;
For welcome, at his hand, were dying.
Why murmur? Nay, I do not; he
Can bring no happiness to me.'

4

But now, attention! march, my story,
Claimed by a novel personage!
Five versts away from Krasnogore,
Lensky's own village, lives in sage
And philosophic rumination
And in rude health, in isolation,
Even now, Zaretsky: – ruffian,
Of gambling gangs once ataman,
A pothouse tribune, lord of riot;
But now the kindly, simple head
And sire of children (though unwed);
A trusted friend, a landlord quiet;
Nay, man of honour! Thus, in brief,
Our age turns over a new leaf!

5

Time was, the world would loudly flatter
And laud his bitter courage; true,
He with a pistol-ball could shatter
An ace, twelve yards away, clean through.
And true it is that once, while fighting,
He won his honours by delighting
Fairly in battle; he was bold
When from his Kalmuck steed he rolled,
Sotlike, in mud: – the French had seized him
(Rare prize!), this latest Regulus,
In honour like a god; for thus
To re-surrender greatly pleased him,
If, every morn, at Verrey's,[1] he
Might drain (on credit) bottles three.

6

His banter – once it was amusing:
For publicly, or on the sly,
Fools he loved duping and confusing,
And fooled the clever, splendidly.
Some tricks, no doubt, had not succeeded,
But taught him lessons badly needed,
And sometimes he would slip into
A scrape, as common noodles do.
Well could he, skilled in disputation,
Give answers blunt, or barbs that stung,
By calculation, hold his tongue,
Or goad by equal calculation
His younger friends to wrath, and bring
Them on the ground, for duelling,

7

Or, to make peace he would induce them;
Then they would breakfast, all the three;
Next, he would stealthily traduce them
With gay, mendacious pleasantry.
Sed alia tempora! such daring
Frolics, like love's young dream, are wearing
Away with lively youth, and fade.
My friend Zaretsky, as I said,
Beneath his cherries and acacias
At last from storms and tempests hides
And like a true wise man abides
And plants his cabbage, like Horatius,
Content his ducks and geese to breed,
Teaching his children how to read.

8

No fool was he: Yevgeny, rating
Meanly his qualities of heart,
Yet liked his tone in estimating,
And good sound sense he would impart
On this and that; was wont to meet him,
Till now, with pleasure; and to greet him
This morning suffered no surprise
Now, when Zaretsky met his eyes;
– Who, with the words of welcome over,
Broke off the talk, and with a grim
Smirk on his face, delivered him
A missive from the poet-lover.
Onegin to the window flew,
And to himself he read it through.

9

It was an honourable, pleasing
Cartel, or challenge: brief, polite,
And unmistakeable, and freezing;
Lensky called out his friend – to fight.
To him who brought this dire proposal
Onegin turning, '*At disposal*
Always', on impulse then declared,
Saying no word that might be spared.
Zaretsky rose, without explaining;
To tarry longer he declined
– He'd many things at home to mind –
And sped. Yevgeny, now remaining
Alone, with his own soul must hide,
Still with himself dissatisfied;

10

– And justly: strict examination
Of conscience, in her private dock,
Showed many a cause for accusation.
First, he'd been in the wrong to mock,
Last evening, in his heedless fashion,
So shy and delicate a passion;
And next: – the poet might have been
Too foolish; still, at just eighteen,
'Twas venial; and Yevgeny, loving
That youth with all his heart, should show
He was no ball tost to and fro
By prejudice, but should be proving
A man of honour, one who had
Wisdom; no hot, pugnacious lad.

11

He could have well disclosed his feeling,
Not bristled like a beast at bay;
And to that young, soft heart appealing,
Should have disarmed it. But today
The time was past, and he belated;
Besides, Yevgeny meditated,
That old, bad, loose-tongued, gossiping
Swordsman had meddled with the thing.
His funny talk – no doubt we'd hold it
Contemptible, but whisper rules,
That, and the snickering of fools;
Public opinion, too – behold it![2]
– Our idol – honour's mainspring! lo,
The axis of this world below!

12

The poet, for his answer staying
At home, is chafing – seethes with hate;
Behold, the answer now conveying,
His garrulous neighbour comes, in state!
Great feast-day for the jealous lover!
That trickster now could not discover
A loophole, or by some shrewd jest
Avert the pistol from his breast,
As Lensky had been deeply fearing.
For now all doubts are laid, and they
Must by the mill at break of day
Upon the morrow be appearing,
And then, with pistols cocked, let fly
Each at the other's brow, or thigh.

13

Lensky – still boiling – had intended
To loathe his Olga, that coquette;
Would shun her, till the fray was ended;
He scanned both sun and watch; and yet
Soon he had given up these labours
And driven round to see his neighbours.
He thought that Olga, when he came,
Would be confused, and sink for shame;
But no such thing: dear Olga, greeting
Our luckless bard as usual, there
Skipt in high spirits down the stair,
Like Hope on airy pinions fleeting;
Was carefree, gay; in truth, I mean,
Was just what she had always been.

14

‘And why, last night, were you concealing
Yourself so early?’ Olga said
Forthwith. Distraught with many a feeling,
Lensky was silent, hung his head.
That clear and candid gaze had banisht
All jealousy; chagrin had vanisht
Before that simple, tender mien,
That soul so sprightly and so keen . . .
And he, with sweet emotion thrilling,
Looked, saw that he was loved; and hence,
Now pining in deep penitence,
To crave her pardon he was willing;
Yet, trembling, found no words, assured
That he was happy – all but cured . . .

(15, 16^3) 17

Downcast, and in dejection falling
Once more, – with darling Olga there
His tongue would have no part in calling
Her thoughts to yesterday’s affair;
And he reflected, ‘I shall save her;
I will not let that wretch deprave her;
He shall not tempt her youthful heart
With sighs and flames, and flattering art!
The poisonous worm that I am scorning
My lily’s stem shall not gnaw through,
Nor that half-budded floweret new
Fade, ere it twice has seen the morning.’
– And, sirs, all this but meant one thing:
‘My friend, and I, go pistolling.’

18

Had he but known the wound, the fever
Consuming Tanya's heart away;
Had Tanya known, or could she ever
Have had the power to know, how they,
Those friends, tomorrow would be spending,
To win a shadowy grave contending;
Perhaps the love she harboured might
Have brought those friends to reunite!
But none by chance had yet detected
The passion that within her stirred;
Onegin uttered never a word;
Tanya in secret pined, dejected;
And no one but the nurse could know;
And she was dull of brain, and slow.

19

And Lensky, he was absent-minded,
First mute, then bright, the evening through.
These Muses' nurslings, as I find it,
Are all alike! At times he drew
Up to the harpsichord, and sitting,
Struck casual chords, his eyebrows knitting;
Or gazed on Olga, murmuring, 'This
Is surely true, is surely bliss?'
But now 'twas late, and time for taking
Departure; – while farewell he bade
To that young girl, his heart was sad,
Full-charged, and pent, and felt like breaking.
She scans his face: 'What ails you? say.'
'Nothing!' And so, downstairs, away!

20

Then Lensky, to his home proceeding,
Saw to his pistols; put them back
Into the case; undressed; tried reading
Schiller by candle-light. – Alack,
One, one beleaguering thought assails him;
His heart is sore, and slumber fails him;
For still, unutterably fair,
He seems to see his Olga there.
Vladimir then, the volume closing,
Takes up his pen: his verses teem
With lovers' babble; in a stream
They flow, they ring; and he, composing,
With lyric fire declaims the lines,
Like drunken Delvig when he dines.

21

I have his poem; you shall read it;
For, as it chanced, they saved the thing:
– 'Ah, whither have ye now receded,
Whither, my golden days of spring?
For me, what is the morrow storing?
How vainly is my gaze exploring!
All, all is wrapt in misty night.
No need: for Fate will judge aright.
Whether I fall, a bullet through me,
Whether it miss, I still am blest.
The hour to wake, or hour to rest,
Will come, the hour allotted to me.
Blest, if the day to labour calls;
Blest also, if the darkness falls.

22

'Yes, though the morning ray be sparkling
And day dawn brilliant, yet shall I
Be entering, perhaps, the darkling
Grave, with its shadowy mystery;
And tardy Lethe soon shall cover
The name of the young poet-lover.
The world will not remember me.
– But thou, fair maiden, thou wilt be
By my untimely urn, and by it
Wilt weep, and muse, "His love was great;
To me alone was consecrate
The sad morn of a life unquiet."
– Friend of my heart, for whom I sigh,
Come to me, come! thy spouse am I.'

23

This penned he, in the *dark, faint* fashion
We style 'romantic' – though I see
No feature of romantic passion
Therein – but it concerns not me.
At last, before the dawn came gleaming,
Upon the word *ideal* dreaming
(The word in vogue) he drooped his head
For weariness, and drowsed in bed.
Scarce in oblivion was he falling
Of blissful sleep – his neighbour broke
Into the silent room, and woke
Our Lensky from his slumbers, calling
'Time you were up! by now, be sure,
Onegin waits; 'tis seven, and more.'

24

But he mistook: Yevgeny's sleeping
As sleep the dead; already far
The thinner shades of night are creeping
And cocks salute the morning star.
The sun wheels high in heaven; yet soundly
Yevgeny sleeps, – and more profoundly.
A storm of snow comes fleeting past
And glitters in the whirling blast.
Still, sleep above Yevgeny hovers,
Still, on the pillow lies his head . . .
But then – at last! – he's out of bed.
The curtained windows he uncovers,
Peers out – and sees beyond all doubt
It is high time he sallied out.

25

He rings in haste; and in comes flying
Guillot, his lackey and a Gaul,
Slippers and dressing-gown supplying,
And change of linen brings withal.
Onegin swiftly then attires him,
And bids the man prepare; requires him
To drive with him, and bring away
The case of weapons for the fray.
The sledge stands ready; off he courses,
And in it to the mill they tear.
Behind him must the lackey bear
Lepage's[4] deadly arms; the horses
Are driven to a plot of land
Apart, where two oak saplings stand.

26

Lensky impatiently had waited
Long, as he leaned upon the weir.
Zaretsky low the millstones rated
(He was a rustic engineer).
Onegin comes, and brings excuses:
'But,' cries Zaretsky, 'Where the deuce is
Your second?' – As a duellist
He was a pedant, would insist
On classic forms; of all things dearest
To him was method; he'd allow
Your man to drop – not anyhow
But on the principles severest
Of art, in old tradition's ways
(Which, in Zaretsky, we must praise).

27

'Where,' says Onegin, 'is my second?
Monsieur Guillot, my friend, is here,
Whom I present. I had not reckoned
Upon demurs. He is, I'm clear,
– Though not a man of note, I grant it –
An honest soul. What more is wanted?'
Zaretsky bit his lip, and heard;
And then Onegin spoke a word
To Lensky: 'Well, shall we get started?'
'Yes,' said Vladimir, 'if you will.'
And so they stept behind the mill.
The 'honest soul' some way departed
With grave words to Zaretsky; fast
The foes now stand, with gaze downcast.

28

– Foes! and how long had this estranging
Bloodthirstiness between them flared?
How long since, all their thoughts exchanging,
Their leisure hours as friends they shared,
Their meals, their doings? Evil-hearted,
As though by hate ancestral parted,
In calm cold blood they now prepare
To kill each other, as it were
In some insensate, dreadful vision.
And why not part in friendship, ere
Their hands are red – and only care
To laugh the matter to derision?
– But false and foolish shame intrudes
Its terrors in our worldly feuds.

29

Behold, the pistols now are gleaming;
The hammer on the ramrod knocks;
Down the cut barrels now are streaming
The bullets; once, have snapt the cocks;
And now the greyish powder scatters
Into the pan, and down it spatters.
The jagged flints, screwed safe below,
Are lifted still. – There stands Guillot
Behind a stump, in consternation.
The fighters cast their cloaks; the due
Paces, in number thirty-two,
Zaretsky, with due mensuration.
Has taken. At the further ends
With pistols drawn he plants the friends.

30

'Approach!' – and regularly, coldly,
Not aiming yet, the combatants,
Without a sound, but stepping boldly,
March on; four paces they advance,
Four fatal paces those! Not waiting,
And never his advance abating,
Yevgeny is the first to lift
His pistol, quietly. – They shift
Five paces nearer; Lensky closes
An eye, the left – begins to aim
Also; Onegin at the same
Instant has fired. Thus fate disposes,
And strikes the hour. The poet lets
His pistol drop – his hand he sets

31

Hard to his bosom, never saying
One word, and falls – his clouded eye
No pang, but death itself portraying.
Thus, on a mountain, from on high
A heap of snow may slide, declining
Slowly, with sunny sparkles shining.
Then, on a sudden stricken cold,
Onegin rushes to behold
The youth, all vainly on him calling.
But he is gone; and he who sung
Has ended all too soon, too young.
One blast – and the fair blossom falling
All withered now, at daybreak, lies;
The flame upon the altar dies!

32

He lay, he stirred not; what strange reading,
That peace and languor on his brow!
The wound that still was steaming, bleeding,
Pierced clean below the breast. Even now,
A moment since, with inspiration
That heart had throbbed, with animation
Of hope, of love, of enmity.
The blood seethed hot, the life beat high.
And now, just like a house deserted,
All dark and still it has become,
Has fallen for ever mute and dumb;
The shutters up, the windows dirtied
With wiped-on chalk. No host is there,
For she has vanisht – God knows where!

33

'Tis sweet to drive your foe unwary
Wild, with a jaunty epigram;
To watch that stubborn adversary
Just lowering his horns to ram;
He sees his face; for shame he knows it;
Too surely now that mirror shows it!
And sweeter still, my friends, if he,
The fool, be howling, 'Why, that's me!'
Nay, sweeter still to make him ready
A grave of honour – decent space
Allowing, at his blanching face
Taking a quiet aim and steady.
And yet – to send the man to meet
His fathers – *that* you'll scarce find sweet.

34

Your ball – imagine, if you can, sir –
Has slain a youth, one of your friends,
Who by some trifle, some wrong answer
Or saucy leering, caused offence
Over the wine. Or he, impatient,
In burning pride and indignation,
Himself the fateful challenge threw.
What feeling, say, o'ermastering you,
Will fill your soul, when that still figure
There on the ground, before your eyes
With death upon its forehead lies,
While slow creeps on the mortal rigour?
While he is tarrying silent there,
Deaf to your summons of despair?

35

Yevgeny, gripping pistol tightly,
Filled with compunction, now in dread
On Lensky looks. His neighbour lightly
Pronounces, 'That's it, then. He's dead.'
'Dead!' As that hideous word is sounded,
Yevgeny shudders, whelmed, confounded;
Goes off, and calls his men; while there,
The ice-cold body, with due care,
Zaretsky in the sledge is setting.
He drives the ghastly burden home;
The horses scent the dead; with foam
The steely mouthpiece they are wetting;
They rear and struggle, snort and blow,
Then fly, like arrows from the bow.

36

Friends, for our poet you are grieving:
For in the bloom of hope and joy,
Nor yet, before the world, achieving,
Nay, scarce unswaddled still, the boy
Has droopt and died. That warm emotion,
That young and nobly-toucht devotion
To lofty thoughts, to feelings fair,
Gallant, and tender, these are – where?
Where are love's stormy aspirations,
The thirst for knowledge and for toil,
The dread of shame, of deeds that soil,
Where are the hallowed meditations,
The sacred dreams of poetry,
Those tokens of transcendency?

37

And he, perhaps, was born to better
And bless the world; to fame, at worst,
His lyre, now silent, the begetter
Of some unbroken, thunderous burst
Of sacred song? A poet fated
To be on some high place awaited
Of the world's stairway? Has his shade
That suffered much, away conveyed
Some holy secret? Quencht for ever,
That voice life-giving, in our ears?
His shade no psalm of ages hears;
The blessings of mankind shall never
Now reach him in their flight, or come
Beyond the borders of the tomb.

(38^5) 39

But yet our poet, I admit it,
Might have some common lot fulfilled.
His years of youth might soon have flitted,
The soul within quickly chilled;
He might have greatly changed, and married;
No longer with the Muses tarried;
Happy, within the country's bournes,
Wearing his dressing-gown – and horns,
He would have known what life is truly;
At forty, would have had the gout,
Drunk, fed, moped, pined, and fattened out;
At last, and in his bed, would duly,
While doctors gazed, and women cried,
With all his children round – have died.

40

Reader, howe'er it be, we know it,
Alas! that lover young lies low,
That pensive, visionary poet,
Whose friend had dealt the murderous blow.
– Left of the village, habitation
Once of that child of inspiration,
There is a spot: – two firs have twined
Their roots; beneath them runlets wind,
Down from a neighbour valley lipping;
And there the ploughman loves to rest,
And women-reapers come in quest
Of water, resonant pitchers dipping;
And by that streamlet, in deep shade,
A simple monument is laid.

41

Beneath it (when the meadow grasses
The early springtime rain bedews)
Singing of Volga fishers, passes
The shepherd, plaiting motley shoes,[6]
And the young city girl, abiding
A summer in the country, riding
And starting, all alone, to fly
Along the plain impetuously,
Will pull her leathern bridle tightly,
And halt her horse before the place,
And from her hat the veil unlace,
And read the simple legend, lightly
Skimming the words; and tears will rise,
And cloud the lady's gentle eyes.

42

Then on the open plain, and slowly,
Plunged in long reverie, she goes,
And Lensky's destiny must wholly,
Like it or not, her soul engross.
She muses: 'What of Olga, surely?
Did her heart suffer long and sorely,
Or dried her tears too rapidly?
And where may now her sister be?
And where that man of mode, who fleeing
The world of men, detested too
Fair modish women, and who slew
The youthful poet? Strange, grim being!'
Well, in good time I shall not fail
All this to answer in detail;

43

Not now! I hold in warm affection
My hero; and I shall, I vow,
To him return; but on reflection,
My mood is not for him just now.
To hard prose call the years that vanish;
Frolicsome rhyme the same years banish
And much less eagerly do I
Now court her. (Saying which, I sigh).
No more my pen is bent on soiling
Ephemeral folios, as of old;
For other dreams – alas, too cold –
Find me at sterner labours toiling:
In the world's din, or silence deep,
They trouble still my soul, in sleep.

44

I've found a different way of grieving,
But still the ancient grief regret;
My first desires I've found deceiving;
But others called – I hear them yet.
Where is your sweetness, dreams untruthful?
Where that eternal rhyme, of *youthful*?
And has youth's garland now at last
Faded, ay, faded, in the past?
And has, in sober fact, and quitting
All mournful fancies, as, till now,
In jest I often would avow, –
The springtide of my days been flitting?
And is it truly past recall?
Am I soon thirty, after all?

45

My noontide, yes, has come; I find it
Must be confessed; I see it well.
But be it so; to youth light-minded,
I say as to a friend, farewell!
I thank you for delights and gladness,
For all sweet torments, and for sadness,
For storms and clamours, banquetings,
And all the gifts your season brings;
I thank you; both in agitation
And in calm hours, I have enjoyed
You to the full – and have been cloyed.
Enough! today, for relaxation,
Clear-souled, I start on courses new,
Bidding that former life adieu.

46

One last look round. Farewell, far places
Of my lost days. Away they stole,
With sloth and passion as their basis
And sweet dreams of a pensive soul.
I beg you, youthful inspiration,
Come, stir up my imagination,
Quicken my slumbering heart, and look
More frequently into my nook.
Let not my poet's soul be captured
By age and callousness alone
And finally be turned to stone,
By the world's deadening joys enraptured,
Sunken, my friends, in that mean slough
Where you and I are wallowing now!

Chapter Seven

Moscow, beloved daughter of Russia, where find thy equal?

DMITRIEV

How not love Moscow, our own?

BARATYNSKY

'You run down Moscow? why of travel make such fuss?
Where better?' – 'Where there's none of us.'[1]

GRIBOYEDOV

I

The radiance of spring is chasing
The snow from the surrounding hills;
Snows to the flooded leas come racing
Down from a hundred turbid rills.
Bright-smiling nature dreams, and meeting
The year's new morning, gives her greeting;
And bluer now the heavens gleam;
The woodlands, still transparent, seem
A down of greenery to be wearing;
The bees wing from their waxen comb,
And levy from the meads bring home;
The drying dales new tints are wearing;
The herds are loud; the nightingale
Warbles, at dead of night, her tale.

2

Spring, spring, love's season! yet how dreary
For me, to see thee round again!
Spring makes me agitated, weary
In spirit, and in every vein.
Ah, what a soft oppressive feeling
Delights me now, when, softly stealing,
The airs of springtime fan my face,
Lapt in this quiet country place!
Is it that all delights forsake me,
And that each bright, exultant thing,
All life, all joyance, can but bring
Ennui, and only weary make me,
Because my soul died long ago
And finds that all is dark? Even so?

3

Or that we only think of sadness
And loss, when perished leaves revive
From autumn, and we feel no gladness
At woodland sounds, once more alive?
Or does our troubled spirit, viewing
Great Nature, still her youth renewing,
Contrast her with *our* years, that fast
Fade in the unreturning past?
Perhaps poetic meditation
Brings fresh into our memory
Some other spring of days gone by
And fills our hearts with agitation
And dreams of some far land, a night
Miraculous in deep moonlight?

4

Now is the time. Good men, you idlers,
Wise sons of Epicurus, cool
And lucky, fancy-free and mindless,
You fledglings of the Levshin[2] school,
You rural Priams, and you gentle
Ladies, now feeling sentimental,
The spring invites you all to hours
Of country labour, and to flowers,
Inspiring strolls, and warmer weather,
And the allurements of the night.
So hasten, friends, with all your might
To fields, in chaises packed together,
Go post, or hire your nags, nor wait,
But speed you from the city gate.

5

And you, kind reader, now forsaking
The town and all its turbulence,
The scene of winter's merrymaking,
Bespeak your coach, and hurry hence.
Come with my muse – no mistress firmer –
And hear with me the oak-trees murmur
Over some stream without a name,
Where, for a country winter, came
Of late Yevgeny, a sick-hearted
And idle hermit – and a near
Neighbour, as well, to her, my dear
Young dreaming Tanya. He, departed,
Although no more they see his face,
Has left his melancholy trace.

6

Come, let us see the brooklet winding
Beneath half-circling hillsides, fast
Down through the linden grove, and finding
The river by green fields at last.
Here chants the nightingale, spring's lover,
All night, and where the blossoms cover
The briar, and bubbling waters call,
Here stands a stone funereal
Beneath two pine-trees antiquated.
The legend tells the passer-by,
'Vladimir Lensky here doth lie';
(The year, his age, are duly dated.)
'Too soon he died, as die the brave;
Have peace, young poet, in thy grave'.

7

Time was, above that urn so quiet,
Once a mysterious garland hung
Upon the sagging pine-tree by it
And in the breeze of morning swung.
Time was two friends, two women, hither
Would come, at leisure, late, together
And in the moonlight vigil keep
And by the tomb embrace, and weep.
Now is that stone, forlorn and lonely,
Forgot; the trodden track is now
O'ergrown; no wreath is on the bough.
Beneath the monument now, only
The frail, gray shepherd sings his songs
And plaits his shoes from wretched thongs.

(8, 9[3]) 10

Ah, my poor Lensky! Olga's weeping
And pining were not long to pass.
His young betrothed soon changed, not keeping
Faith with her sorrow; for, alas,
Another came, her mind alluring,
By lover's flatteries ensuring
That all her pangs should be appeased.
A Lancer charmed, a Lancer pleased;
Her soul adored him; and already
Behold her bashful, by his side,
With drooping head, and crowned a bride,
Before the altar standing steady;
Her lips smile softly, and there flies
A sparkle from the downcast eyes.

11

Ah, my poor Lensky! Heard you, dwelling
In that deaf tomb, eternity,
These fateful tidings, clearly telling
An anguished bard how false was she?
Or does our poet, now possessing
The drowsy Lethe's supreme blessing,
Feel nothing, of all trouble rid?
Is this world dumb to him, and hid? . . .
Yes, past the grave there lies before us
Heedless oblivion, in the end;
The voice of mistress, foe, and friend
Dies swiftly; and the wrathful chorus
Of our unseemly, wrangling heirs
Just for our goods and chattels cares.

12

Soon, Olga's voice no more resounded
Clear in the Larins' home; she went,
When, duty's slave, her Lancer found it
Needful to join his regiment.
Her ageing mother, at her going,
With bitter tears was overflowing.
She said goodbye, and seemed half-dead.
But Tanya had no tears to shed:
Her face of misery was shrouded
With deathly pallor. When at last
All to the outer stairway passed
And round the young folks' carriage crowded
In farewell bustle – then, indeed,
She saw them off, and gave godspeed.

13

And long Tatyana traced them, straining
Her gaze as through a mist . . . Alas,
She is alone, alone remaining!
Into the distance now must pass,
Swept off by destiny, her dearest,
The friend of years, of all the nearest
Unto her bosom, her young dove,
Parted for ever from her love.
Now, aimless like a shadow straying,
She glances at the garden bare . . .
No comfort here, none anywhere!
Her eyes can shed no tears allaying
Her grief. She stifles them in vain,
For Tanya's heart is rent in twain.

14

And higher mounts her passion, glowing
In this fell solitude; today
Her heart speaks all the louder, knowing
Onegin now is far away.
For nevermore shall she behold him;
She ought to hate him, and to hold him
As one who has her brother slain.
Lost is that poet! none remain
Who think of *him*; his bride has given
Her hand, unto another wed.
The poet's memory has fled
Like vapour in an azure heaven.
Two hearts, maybe, are still forlorn
And mourn for him . . . Yet, wherefore mourn?

15

The evening skies are dark, and flowing
Gently, the brooks; the beetles hum;
The rings of dancers home are going;
Smoke, flame across the river come
From fishers' fires. And Tanya yonder
Goes in the open fields to wander
Beneath the silver moonlight's beams,
Buried for ever in her dreams.
Alone, and ever onward pacing,
Now from a little knoll she sees
A village and a clump of trees;
The master's house; a clear stream racing
Below a garden. Here at last!
Her heart beats heavily and fast.

16

But doubts and questionings beset her.
'Go back? Go forward? Which is worst?
They know me not – he's absent – better
Just see the house and garden first!'
So Tanya, from the knoll descending
Now breathless, and her full gaze bending
On all around her, passes next
To the deserted court, perplext.
The dogs come barking, charging at her,
And, at her shriek of terror, out
The servants' children with a shout
Rush, and with scuffle and with clatter
The hounds they hustle from the yard
And take the lady under guard.

17

She asks them, 'May I not look over
The master's house?' The children flee
To ask Anisya, to discover
And from the passage take the key.
Anisya straight appears before her;
And then the doors fly open for her.
Into our hero's empty home,
Where late he dwelt, is Tanya come.
She sees, as through the hall she glances,
Reposing, a forgotten cue;
Upon the tumbled sofa, too,
A riding crop. Now she advances.
'Here is the hearth,' said the old crone.
'The master sat here all alone.

18

'And poor late Mr Lensky, dining
In wintertime, was oft his guest.
(This way – please follow.) Here, reclining
At night, the master used to rest.
(This is his den.) His coffee taking
He'd listen to the bailiff making
Reports; and, in the morning, read.
– Old Master too lived here, indeed:
On Sundays too, wearing his glasses,
Just by the window here would he
Deign to be playing cards with me;
God save his soul, and grant his ashes
Peace in the grave, in the damp earth,
Mother from whom he had his birth.'

19

Tatyana stands afflicted, gazing
On what surrounds her here; the whole
Seems like a treasure past appraising,
And quickens now her weary soul
With solace half-excruciating:
– A quenched lamp on the table waiting,
Books piled and, by the window set,
A small bed with its coverlet,
A window view with moonlight solemn
Shedding a pale half-light on all,
Lord Byron's portrait on the wall,
A statuette upon a column –
A man with beetling brows, a hat
And tight-crossed arms.[4] She sees all that.

20

Tatyana, in that modish dwelling,
Stood long; like one bewitched she seemed;
'Twas late; a colder breeze was swelling;
The vale was dark; the coppice dreamed
Above the river overclouded;
The moon behind the crest was shrouded;
And long, long since the time had come
For that young pilgrim to go home.
And Tanya masks her agitation,
And, not without a sigh or so,
Upon her backward path must go,
But begs to make a visitation
Of that lone castle, there to brood
Upon the books, in solitude.

21

With the housekeeper by the gateway
Parting, she resolutely came
Again, next morning early, straightway
To that deserted house, the same
Study in silence wrapt; and letting
Her thoughts roam free, the world forgetting,
Tanya was now alone at last;
She shed tears; some long moments passed,
The – to the books, at first unheeding,
Because they were not to her mind:
The choice of them she could but find
A strange one. Yet she fell to reading,
And her soul thirsted; to her view
Opened another world, and new.

22

'Twas long, we know, since our Yevgeny
Misliking all his books began;
Yet there were certain works, not many,
Which he excluded from his ban:
The singer of the Giaour and Juan,
And a romance or two, a new one
In which the age its face might see,
And modern man might also be
With some fair share of truth depicted:
Lacking all moral interest,
Arid of spirit, self-obsessed,
And in excess to dreams addicted;
The bitter, angry cast of thought,
A-boil with deeds – that came to naught.

23

And many a page she saw retaining
The marks his finger-nails once wrote;
As her observant eyes were straining
On these, and taking keener note,
Tanya beheld with trepidation
The style of thought and observation
That struck Yevgeny; she could see
Where he would silently agree;
She scanned the margins, all displaying
His pencil-tracings everywhere,
In which Onegin's soul lay bare,
Unconsciously itself betraying:
Brief words, or crosses, in the books,
Or question-marks with little hooks.

24

And as she read, slowly but really
Tatyana (God be praised, say I!)
Began to understand more clearly
The man who'd cost her many a sigh
(As cruel destiny had fated):
A grievous, dangerous freak, created
Either by heaven or by hell;
A fiend imperious – who shall tell?
Or angel? Just an imitation,
A phantom nothing; or, at best,
Moscow, in *Harold's* mantle drest,
Of foreign whims an illustration?
A modish phrase-book, rich in store?
Nay, a sheer parody, no more?

25

Has she succeeded, then, in hitting
The very *word*? the riddle guessed?
Tanya forgets how time is flitting,
How she's awaited by the rest
At home. Two neighbours there are talking
About her while she stays out walking.
'No child is Tanya! well, what next?'
So the old mother groans, perplext;
'Why, Olga's younger; and time presses;
Yes, yes; she must be settled now.
How deal with her? To all, I vow,
The only thing she bluntly says is
"I won't!" And still she pines, and roves
Alone amongst the woods and groves.'

26

– 'In love, then?' – 'Well, but who's the man, sir?
Refused – the suit Buyanov pressed.
For Petushkov (Ivan), same answer!
And how hussar Pykhtin, a guest
Of ours one day, was fascinated
By Tanya, and himself prostrated!
I thought, with luck, there's hope in this;
But once again things went amiss!'
'A pretty pass; you must unblock it!
Moscow's the place, Moscow provides
A ready market-place for brides.'
'Good sir, I'm rather low in pocket.'
'Enough to see one winter through.
If not, I'll lend some cash to you.'

27

Such blest advice, which stood to reason,
Charmed the old lady. Then and there
Reckoning, she chose the winter season,
When they to Moscow would repair.
Such news! and Tanya came to know it.
The world is exigent: – to show it
For judgment, such clear, patent traits
Of simple and provincial ways;
Her dress, so out of date appearing;
So out of date her turn of speech;
To draw the mocking looks of each
Circe, or fop, of Moscow's rearing:
– Too dreadful! Better far she should
Stay safe, in some sequestered wood.

28

The earliest rays of dawn have found her
Already risen; forth she flies
Into the fields, and gazes round her,
Scanning them all with tender eyes:
'Farewell, you valleys quiet-nested,
And you familiar ranges crested!
Farewell, you woods, familiar too!
Farewell, O lovely, heavenly blue,
And Nature, full of joy and pleasure!
I quit this peace, long dear to me,
For noise and glittering vanity.
Farewell, my freedom, thou my treasure!
Ah, wherefore haste I, to what shore?
What next has fate for me in store?'

29

Tatyana rambles on for ever
And stays her steps against her will.
The fascination of the river
Arrests her, or some little hill.
Her converse she is still prolonging,
As with old friends about her thronging,
With each beloved holt and lea.
But summer fleets too rapidly,
And golden autumn is before us.
Pale Nature quakes, like some elect
Victim, magnificently decked.
The north winds breathe and howl in chorus
And chase the clouds; and now we see
Winter, in all his witchery.

30

He's here! he hangs, in snow-dust flying,
On every oaken bough and bole,
His billowy coverlet now lying
On every field, round every knoll.
See, with his feathery shroud invested,
Flush with its bank the stream arrested.
The frost is sparkling; glad are we
At Father Winter's game and glee.
Tanya alone finds this unmoving;
The winter she is loth to greet,
And breathe the powdery frost and sleet,
Or with new snow from off the roofing
To wash her shoulder, breast, and face;
For Tanya dreads the wintry ways.

31

Long the departure is retarded;
Soon the last moment will be due;
The coach, forgotten and discarded,
Is scanned, made sounder, lined anew.
Three covered sleighs and customary
Carts will the household chattels carry.
And many a jar of jam is there,
Mattress and saucepan, trunk and chair,
And poultry-coop and bed of feather.
Pots, basins, and the rest are found;
Nay, goods of every sort abound.
The servants, in the hut together,
Weep parting tears and raise a shout,
And eighteen nags come trooping out,

32

To draw the master coach. They pile up
Kibitkas mountain-high. A bunch
Of squabbling crones and coachmen file up.
The cooks are off preparing lunch.
A mangy nag, one in a million,
Bears the bewhiskered old postilion,
And servants to the gateway fly
To wish their masters fond goodbye.
All seated! Past the gate comes gliding
The honoured carriage, at a crawl.
'Farewell, lone shelter! Farewell, all
You scenes of quietude abiding!
When shall I see you?' Tanya cries,
And tears, o'erbrimming, flood her eyes.

33

Hereafter, when the limitations
Of our enlightenment, so blest,
(Though philosophic calculations
Predict five hundred years, at least)
Are once removed, our roads, believe it,
Will all be changed. (You can't conceive it!)
And highways, made, will then connect
Russia throughout, and intersect;
Cast iron bridges, arches spacious,
Will all the waters then bestride;
Hills will be moved; those waters wide
Tunnelled beneath, by vaults audacious.
The Christian world will institute
Inns, at all stages on the route.

34

Our roads are now abominable;[5]
Bridges, neglected, rotting lie;
Nor, at the stations, are we able
For bugs and fleas to wink an eye.
Inns there are none; the huts are freezing;
And, vainly still the palate teasing,
Hangs the pretentious bill of fare
With all its hunger-bitten air.
And village blacksmiths Cyclopean
Before a sluggish fire attend
And with their Russian hammers mend
The flimsy hardware European,
And bless the pits and holes that cut
Their native soil, and every rut.

35

Yet nice, in the cold winter season,
And easy 'tis to drive along
Roads smooth – as lines devoid of reason
Or sense in fashionable song.
And our Automedons are clever
And smart; our troikas weary never;
The mile-posts flash, like palings, by,[6]
And entertain the listless eye.
The luckless Larina, affrighted
By costs of posting many a stage,
Crawled in her private equipage;
Whilst our young maiden's soul delighted
In all the tedium of the way.
– And so, seven days and nights, fared they.

36

Nearer and nearer! Now they are gazing
On Moscow, with her stonework white
And ancient cupolas, all blazing
With golden crosses fiery-bright.
Ah, brethren, what contentment filled me
When that swift revelation thrilled me
Of church and belfry, garden, hall
In crescent half-encircling all!
How oft in grief, from thee long parted
Throughout my vagrant destiny,
Moscow, my thoughts have turned to thee!
Moscow . . . what thoughts in each true-hearted
Russian come flooding at that word!
How deep an echo there is heard!

37

There, by its oaken grove surrounded,
Stands Peter's gloomy fort, in state
And pride; of late had glory crowned it.
All vainly must Napoleon wait,
Drunk with his latest, last successes,
Till kneeling Moscow on him presses
Her ancient Kremlin's keys. – Not so!
To him my Moscow would not go,
Head lowered, in capitulation.
No welcoming gift, festivity,
For that impatient hero she
Made ready – but a conflagration;
And thence, deep sunk in thought, he gazed
Upon that menace, as it blazed.

38

Now, Peter's fort, farewell, attesting
Those fallen glories! – Whiter show
The barrier-pillars; now, unresting,
Along Tverskaya let us go.
The coach along the ruts is dashing;
Stalls, countrywomen, by are flashing:
– Watchboxes, children at their play,
Convent and palace, lamp and sleigh,
Bukharian, merchant, Cossack, peasant;
Huts, drugstores, boulevards, and towers,
And gardens both for fruit and flowers;
Shops, telling what's the mode at present;
Balconies, lions topping gates;[7]
And daws, on every cross, in spates.

(39[8]) 40

This weary, long peregrination
Lasts one, two hours; the carriage-train
Halts by a gateway, takes its station
By Kharitonye,[9] in the lane.
Now here they are at last, arriving
At aunty's. She is still surviving,
Consumptive these three years and more.
A gray Kalmuk flings wide the door;
In torn kaftan and specs he meets them,
Holding a stocking. Shrieks arise;
The princess from her salon cries,
And, stretcht along her sofa, greets them.
The ancient ladies weep, embrace,
And exclamations pour apace.

41

'Princess! *Mon ange*!' – 'Pachette! If ever . . .' –
'Alina! What an age!' – 'You'll stay
Some time?' – 'Dear Cousin!' – 'Well I never,
So strange! Good heavens! Be seated, pray!
A scene from the romances, say I!'
– 'My daughter here, Tatyana – may I . . .?'
– 'Ah-h! little Tanya! come, sit here;
It's like a dream! . . . But, cousin dear,
That Grandison – don't you remember?'
– 'What, Grandison? . . . Ah, *Grandison*!
Yes, yes – where's he?' 'To Moscow gone;
Lives by St Simeon.[10] Last December,
On Christmas Eve, he called on me.
Just married off his son, you see;

42

'While *he* – but aren't we, later, going
To tell all that? Tomorrow, we
Tanya to all her kin are showing.
Sad – driving is too much for me,
And my poor feet I'm scarcely dragging.
But come, your journey has been fagging;
We one and all must take a rest . . .
Oh, I am done . . . so tired, my chest!
For joy, these days, weighs hard upon one,
No less than grief . . . Dear soul, I vow
I am just good for nothing now . . .
Life is too vile, as age creeps on one . . .'
And there, exhausted, she breaks off
In tears, and with a racking cough.

43

The sufferer's words, so blithe and loving,
Touch Tanya; yet, accustomed still
To her old room, she finds that moving
To these new quarters suits her ill.
When to a strange bed she betakes her
Beneath silk curtains, sleep forsakes her.
The bells, announcing with their din
That the day's work must now begin,
Make her start up; and so she rises.
But when she stares out through the glass
Through the thin light she sees, alas,
Not fields but only stark surprises –
An unknown courtyard stretching hence,
A stable, kitchen-house and fence.

44

Tanya is taken daily, paying
Visits to kindred to be viewed
By each grandparent – still betraying
Her inattentive lassitude.
The clan, far-travelled, meet with hearty
And welcoming words from every party;
All, offering bread and salt, exclaim:
'How Tanya's grown! It seems I came
To church to act as your godmother
But yesterday.' – 'I carried you.'
'I gave you gingerbread to chew.'
'I pulled your ears.' To one another
The grannies all chant, 'My, oh my!
God save me, how the years do fly!'

45

In *them* no change can be detected;
The ancient pattern holds; oh yes,
The same tulle nightcap is erected
On Aunt Elèna, the princess.
Same ceruse, on Lukerya Lvovna!
Still fibbing is Lyubov Petrovna;
Ivan Petrovich – still not bright;
Semyon Petrovich – still as tight;
And Pelagea changes never
Monsieur Fine-Mouche, her ancient flame;
Her spitz – and husband – still the same;
And he, the punctual clubman ever,
Though just as deaf and quiet still,
Still eats for two – and can he swill!

46

The daughters soon to their embraces
Took Tanya. First, though, they were mute,
This band of Moscow's youthful Graces;
They looked her down from head to foot.
They find her oddish, as they scan her:
Affected, countrified in manner,
And palish too, and leanish; still,
Her looks are very far from ill.
They next (as nature bids) befriend her
And take her to their own abode,
And fluff her curls to suit the mode,
With many a kiss and handclasp tender;
And then, in singsong tones, impart
The secrets of a maiden's heart,

47

Their hopes, their pranks, their meditations,
And others' conquests – and their own.
That stream of guileless conversations
They gloss with light aspersions thrown.
Before long they began inviting
Tanya (their prattle thus requiting)
To bare her heart; but oh, she seems
To move as in a land of dreams:
She hears them talk, and talk – uncaring.
And nothing can she comprehend,
But still in silence will defend
The secret of her heart, not sharing
Her sacred, treasured tears, her bliss:
None shall participate in this!

48

When in the salon, Tanya wishes
To join thc talk, but she does not,
For all she hears is chatter which is
Such common, incoherent rot.
All is so callous, void of colour,
And the backbiting – even duller!
In all this chatter, barren, dry,
– News, questions, gossip – days go by,
From jaded brains no smile evoking;
No scintillating thought will glance
At random, or by happy chance;
No heart thrill, even in play or joking.
Void world, wherein you meet no fool
You can so much as ridicule!

49

Young archivists in swarms, conceited,
On Tanya fix their priggish gaze,
And, in their communings repeated,
With much unkindness her appraise.
One dismal fool, in his dejection,
Finds her a pattern of perfection,
And leans against the door, to make
An elegy, for her sweet sake.
One day, too, Vyazemsky sits by her
There, at a tiresome aunt's, to find
That he can interest her mind.
And onc old fellow, quick to spy her
Beside him, queries, 'Who is she?'
And smooths his wig to symmetry.

50

But where, in long-drawn accents ringing,
Bawls boisterous Melpomene,
And where, her tinselled mantle flinging
Before the frigid throng, stands she;
Where peacefully Thalia drowses
Nor heeds the claps of friendly houses;
– Where young spectators gaze upon
Terpsichore, and her alone
(When you and I were younger fellows,
'Twas thus our leisure that we spent),
On Tanya never there are bent
Lorgnettes of ladies, passing jealous;
No connoisseur of fashion cocks
His glass at her, from stall or box.

51

She's brought to the Sobranye palace;
The crush, excitement, stifling heat.
The candles gleam, the music bellows
For whirling, flashing, dancing feet.
Beauties, apparelled oh! so lightly;
Thronged galleries, all chequered brightly;
A crescent of young girls – alike
Sharply on all the senses strike.
Here, too, sworn dandies are proceeding
To flaunt their waistcoats, brazen airs,
And the lorgnette that listless stares;
And here hussars on leave come speeding,
To show themselves, be loud, make hay,
Shine, captivate and speed away.

52

The night holds many a star entrancing,
And Moscow many a lovely maid;
The moon, though, through the blue advancing,
Leaves her companions in the shade.
But she[11] whom I am now forbearing
To harass with my harp, not daring,
Even like a splendid moon is shown
Mid wives and maids to gleam alone.
With what celestial pride she chances
To light upon the earth at will!
What languor does her bosom fill!
What longing in her lingering glances!
Enough, enough! Be silent, do.
To folly you have paid your due.

53

Mid clamours, bowings, laughter ringing,
Bustle, mazurka, galop, waltz,
Tanya – two aunts beside her clinging –
Unnoticed by a pillar halts,
And looks, but nothing sees – detesting
That world excited and unresting.
She stifles here: her dreams aspire
To live in fields, and to retire
Among her own poor village peasants,
And to that solitary nook
Where runs a bright translucent brook;
To her romances, flowery pleasance,
And those lime-alleys, twilit, dim;
– To where she once set eyes on *him*.

54

But, while her fancies, freely flying,
Neglect the world, the boisterous ball,
Tanya is given a thorough eyeing
By a grave, imposing general.
Now aunty is to aunty winking,
Nudging Tatyana into thinking.
She hears two whispers in her ear:
'Glance to your left there. Quick, my dear!'
'Left? where? and what am I to see there?'
'Well, look! no matter – anyhow!
Before that group – there they are now –
Two still – in uniform? But, he there . . .
He's stept away – his side's to you . . .'
– 'What, that stout general? or who?'

55

Tatyana, dear, congratulations
On victory so promising!
Now I digress, testing your patience,
Lest we forget of whom I sing . . .
But, apropos, two words I owe him: –
A friend, a youth, I sing; I show him
With many a quirk, with many a whim.
Bless my long labour, spent on him,
Thou Epic Muse! To me entrust it,
Thy faithful crook, to guide me: nor
Let my feet rove astray! – No more!
This burden, from my neck I thrust it:
In Classic style (if overdue)
This Introduction comes to you.

Chapter Eight

Fare thee well, and if for ever,
Still for ever fare thee well.

BYRON

1

When in my youth serene I flourished,
And in the school park read my prose,
For Apuleius's I nourished
A taste, but not for Cicero's;
And when, in those spring days, I listened
To the swan's cry, where waters glistened
In valley-bottoms secretly,
Then, first, the Muse appeared to me.
A sudden shaft illuminated
My student's cell; the Muse revealed
A host of youthful schemes concealed.
My boyish joys she celebrated,
And Russia's fame, and, on my part,
The hot dreams of a throbbing heart.

2

The world upon her smiled a greeting,
I soared upon my first success;
And old Derzhavin, now retreating
Graveward, remarked us – stayed to bless . . .[1]

3

But for myself one law declaring,
– To do whate'er my passions choose;
My heart with all the rabble sharing,
Oft would I bring my sprightly Muse
To feasts, loud stormy altercation,
Causing night-watchmen consternation.
In those insensate orgies there
My Muse contributed her share,
And like a Bacchanal she sported –
Quaffed – to the party sang her lays.
The gallants of those vanisht days
Her most tempestuously courted.
Amidst my friends I swelled with pride,
My giddy partner by my side.

4

But I, from these associates breaking,
Fled far. She followed – in my flight
How oft with her affection making
My dumb, blank journey a delight
By tales mysterious, enchanting!
How oft, those crags Caucasian haunting,
Lenore-like, when moon shone bright,
Upon my saddle she would light!
And by Taurida's shore, to hearken
To the sea's voice, the Nereid's soft
Incessant whisper, – ah, how oft
She led me, when night's mist would darken;
Where waves, deep-chiming, ever raise
Their hymn, to the World-Father's praise!

5

The glitter, the loud feasts she wholly
Forgets – the capital is far –
And seeks Moldavia's melancholy
Lone haunts, where nomad races are;
Unto their peaceful tents repairing,
And their shy, wild existence sharing;
– Forgets the tongue, which gods affect,
For scant, outlandish dialect,
And songs on her loved steppe-land chanted.
– A transformation-scene now starts!
In guise a damsel of our parts,
She to my garden is transplanted,
Sad cogitations in her look,
And, in her hand, a small French book.

6

Now will I take my Muse, and guide her
To her first fashionable rout;[2]
Of all those charms the steppes provide her
I'm shy, and jealous, and in doubt.
Through those dense rows aristocratic,
Fops, soldiers, persons diplomatic,
And haughty dames, I see her glide,
Sit softly, gaze on every side,
With all the crash and din delighted,
With glancing dresses, glancing talk;
And then by their young hostess walk
In slow defile the guests invited,
With dark-dressed males round dame
Fitting them like a picture-frame.

7

She likes the ordered conversation,
Well-knit, of oligarchs; and old
Age, mixt with high official station,
And its calm arrogance, so cold.
– But who, in this select and crowded
Meeting, stands mute and overclouded?
He seems a stranger to the throng,
And by him faces flash along
Like rows of tedious apparitions.
Why comes he? On his face is seen
Tormented pride – or is it spleen?
Who is this man? Are my suspicions
Correct – Yevgeny? Even so.
When came he? Was it long ago?

8

Is he the same, or calmed in nature?
Is he still posing, freakishly?
He's back once more – what kind of creature?
What will his next performance be?
What guise will now be his – a canter,
Cosmopolite, or quaker-ranter,
Melmoth, Childe Harold, patriot,
Flaunter of some fresh mask, – or what?
Will he be plain good fellow rated,
Like you and me, and all the rest?
My counsel, anyhow, is best –
To drop that style, quite antiquated.
He's hoaxed the world enough. 'And so
You know Onegin?' 'Yes – and no.'

9

Why must you ever be discussing
Him so ungently? Do we find
That we must ceaselessly be fussing,
Censorious of all mankind?
Do these rash fiery spirits hurt us,
Offend us – nay, do they divert us –
In our self-love, our nullity?
Do wits, too fond of ranging free,
Cramp ours? Are we too often taking
Mere talk, for deeds? – You're dull; are you
Malign and feather-headed too?
Are grave men gravely great things making
Of trash? Are we at home alone
In mediocrity – our own?

10

Blest he, who in due course maturing,
Was young – while he was young; and who,
As years went by, was found enduring
Life's chill, that slowly on him grew;
Who, never curious dreams pursuing,
Nor yet the rabble world eschewing,
At twenty, was a fop, or blade;
At thirty, a good marriage made;
At fifty, all his debts contriving
To clear (and debts of friends) – who came
To office, and to wealth and fame,
Thus calmly, in his turn, arriving;
And all the world repeats, mayhap:
'N. N. is such a splendid chap!'

11

I often think – the thought is grievous –
That youth was granted us in vain.
Our youth did nothing but deceive us;
And we failed her. Grievous again,
That all our finest aspirations
Our freshest dreams and meditations,
In swift succession should decay,
Like autumn leaves that rot away.
– One cannot bear the contemplation
Merely of endless feasts; the sight
Of life as some mere formal rite;
Nor following starchy men of station
In mobs – with whom we share in naught
One single passion, or one thought.

12

Nor can I bear to be subjected
To noisy comments (– you'll applaud –),
Then, for wise people who've reflected,
To represent a freak, or fraud,
Or else a madman miserable,
Or monster, marked with Satan's label,
Or – my own Demon . . .[3] Now again
Onegin occupies my pen.
He'd duelled with his friend, and killed him;
Then lived on, aimless, unemployed,
Aged twenty-six. Soon, leisure cloyed;
Fatigue, with being idle, filled him.
No wife – state service – nought to do!
To nothing could he buckle to.

13

And overmastered was Yevgeny
By that tormenting thing (I mean
That cross, so freely borne by many),
A restless wish for change of scene.
He quitted now his country village,
His lonely woods, his fields for tillage,
Where, every day, before him stood
That Shadow, still bestained with blood;
– Began his purposeless migrations,
And to all feelings lockt his breast
But one; – with all things bored, at best,
Was bored with these peregrinations.
He came like Chatsky[4] home withal,
Straight from the boatdeck to the ball.

14

A tremor stirs the throng now, just as
A murmur rustles through the hall.
A lady moves towards the hostess,
Leading a stately general,
A lady all sedately walking.
She's neither cold, nor prone to talking;
Crude glances she will not extend
To all, nor to 'success' pretend.
Her features show no mincing grimace,
No studied tricks, no apery;
Placid and down-to-earth is she,
Advancing like the living image
Of *comme il faut* (– sorry, Shishkov,[5]
A phrase there's no translation of).

15

The ladies move towards her, nearer;
Old dames are beaming at her, too.
The men bow lower, to revere her,
Angling to keep her eyes in view.
The maidens move more softly, drifting
Before her down the room. Uplifting
His nose, his shoulders, topping all,
Strides her supporting general.
No-one would call her a true beauty,
Yet in her no-one ever saw,
From head to foot, the slightest flaw
Which (paying fashion her strict duty)
Those London circles known as high
Might see as '*vulgar*'. Not that I . . .[6]

16

This fine word, which defies translation,
Much as I love it, has remained
Meanwhile, with us, an innovation
And scarce to honour has attained,
Though epigrams find it worth mention . . .
But now my lady claims attention:
So dear, so charming and carefree,
There at the table now is she
By brilliant Voronskaya sitting,
Our Neva's Cleopatra. Still,
All Nina's marble beauty will
(I can imagine you admitting)
Never, for all its dazzling pride,
Eclipse the neighbour at her side.

17

'Can this, can this be she?' asks musing
Yevgeny; 'no . . . it is . . . and yet . . .
From that remote steppe hamlet? . . .' Using
Next his importunate lorgnette,
He scans her face each moment, falling
On features foggily recalling
Those lost from memory long ago.
' – Prince, tell me – you must surely know
Who, in the raspberry beret yonder
Talks with the Spanish Envoy there?'
And the Prince answers, with a stare,
'So long a stranger? Ha! No wonder . . .
But wait, I shall present you. Stay!'
'Who *is* she, though?' 'My wife, I say!'

18

'You're married! Till today I knew not!
How long? . . .' – 'These two years.' – 'My dear sir,
To whom?' – 'A Larina.' – 'You do not
Mean to Tatyana?' – 'You know her?'
'We're neighbours!' – 'Come with me!' Preceding,
The prince towards his wife is leading
His friend and kinsman. The princess
Regards Onegin . . . None the less,
Whate'er embarrassment dismayed her,
Whatever shock her soul might feel,
Whate'er astonishment conceal,
Yet there was nothing that betrayed her;
The same high breeding still she wore,
And bowed, as tranquil as before.

19

And she not only did not shiver
Or flush, or suddenly turn white;
I swear, her eyebrow did not quiver;
Not even were her lips drawn tight.
Onegin – none could scan her over
More studiously – could not discover
One trace of the old Tanya there.
He tried to talk with her – but ne'er
Could he begin! 'Had he been staying
Long here?' she askt him; 'whence came he?
From *their* parts, surely, he must be?'
Then to her spouse she turned, betraying
A weary glance – slipt off for good,
And left him planted where he stood.

20

Was this Tatyana – who'd believe it? –
Whom once, when our romance began,
In that remote, dull spot – conceive it! –
Long since, alone with her, the man,
Full of the blessed glow of preaching,
Had been admonishing and teaching?
She, in whose letter, cherished still,
Her heart had spoken, of free will,
With utter frankness? was he dreaming?
That ungrown girl – could this be she,
Whom, in her modest station, he
Had in those days been disesteeming?
Had *she* encountered him, just now,
With that indifferent, fearless brow?

21

He left the crush, and meditated
Profoundly, on his homeward way;
And dreams disturbed his sleep belated;
Half charming, and half sad, were they.
He wakes: a letter now is brought him;
Prince N. most humbly has besought him
To spend the evening. 'Heavens! I'll see
Her! – I will go!' Politely he
Scrawls a swift answer. What is working
Within him? What strange dream is this?
What is it stirs, in the abyss
Of that cold, listless spirit lurking?
Vexation? Vanity? In truth,
It might be love, that scourge of youth.

22

Once more, he counts the hours that dally,
And chafes, once more, till day shall end.
The clock strikes ten; behold him sally –
Fly – and the outer stair ascend –
And enter, full of trepidation,
To find the princess. At her station
Tatyana waits, alone; the pair
Some minutes sit together there.
Upon his lips the words are dying;
Awkward and sullen he, distraught,
Gives barest answers; one fixt thought
His stubborn brain is occupying;
And fixedly he scans her; she
Sits unconstrained, sits quietly.

23

The husband, presently arriving,
Breaks this unpleasing *tête-à-tête*.
He and Onegin chat, reviving
Old pranks – old jokes reiterate
With laughter. In the guests are streaming;
And conversation quickens, teeming
With worldly malice, salted high;
The hostess sees the sparkles fly,
Light stuff, not silly or affected,
But broken now and then by gleams
Of sense – on sound, not trivial themes
(Though truths eternal are neglected).
Such talk, unpriggish, free, and bright,
No ears could possibly affright.

24

But here were Petersburg's picked gentry,
Servants of fashion and her rules,
Folk who had everywhere the entry,
And – unavoidably – the fools.
Ladies were here – no youthful Graces –
Capped, rose-bedeckt, with bitter faces;
And here some damsels, who by chance
Wore an unsmiling countenance;
Here, too, an Envoy, talking ever
Of some imperial affair;
And here, with grizzled, scented hair,
An old man, passing keen and clever,
Was jesting, in the ancient style
Today so apt to raise a smile.

25[7]

One gentleman, who loves sharp phrases,
Is most irate, finds all things vile;
'Her tea's too sweet!' and he appraises
The women – 'flat!' – the men – 'no style!'
'Why of that hazy novel chatter?
The sisters' monogram?[8] What matter?'
He blames the war – lies pressmen tell –
The snow – and his own wife, as well . . .

26

Prolazov, that base soul, well earning
His reputation – there was he,
Who in each album had been learning
To blunt your pencil-ends, St Priest!
Another stringent ballroom-colonel
Stood, like a picture from a journal
Or a Palm-Sunday cherub, red,
Stiff, dumb, and motionless like lead.
A bird of passage, travelling fleetly,
Starched, insolent, from top to toe;
His studious deportment so
Caused all the guests to smile discreetly
That all condemned him; all, askance
Would interchange a silent glance.

27

Yet my Onegin was but thinking
Of Tanya, that whole evening through:
– No more the lovesick damsel, shrinking
And poor and simple, whom he knew,
But now a proud princess, who cared not;
The goddess – whom approach he dared not –
Of Neva's rich, imperial stream.
O mortals, everywhere you seem
Like Eve, progenitress so distant!
Free gifts do not temptation make;
To that mysterious Tree the Snake
Still summons you, with voice insistent.
That fruit forbidden – hand it o'er,
Or Eden – Eden is no more.

28

Tatyana – what a transformation!
How firmly schooled to play her part!
The crushing manner of her station;
How swiftly she had learnt her part!
This stately, careless lady, maker
Of ballroom statute – who would take her
For that young, gentle miss? He told
Himself, 'I touched her heart, of old';
And in the dark she had regarded
The moon, up-gazing; for his sake
Her maiden heart had learned to ache,
While Morpheus' flight was still retarded;
Dreaming that they might walk one day
Together down life's humble way.

29

At every age, Love finds a servant;
But to young, virgin hearts will bring
Most blessing when impuslive, fervent,
Like tempests to the fields in spring.
The rains of passion driving through them
Bring them to ripeness, and renew them.
Life's virtue, potent at the root,
Is rich in flower and sweet in fruit.
But when slow time and sterile ageing
Take all our years and turn the scale,
Dead passions leave a hapless trail,
Just as the autumn tempests, raging,
Turn meadows soggy everywhere
And leave the woodlands standing bare.

30

Ah, doubt no more! with boy-like passion
Yevgeny is in love; all day,
All night, he pines in lover's fashion
And muses on Tatyana; nay,
Heedless of reason's stern reproaches,
Daily her stairway he approaches,
Her entrance-hall, her window-pane,
A dogging shadow in her train.
And happy he, to be adjusting
The downy boa flung around
Her neck; if his hot hand be found
Just touching hers; or if he's thrusting
Through mobs of motley liveries – all
For her – or picking up her shawl.

31

But she, for all his struggles, never
Once marks him (he may die – or live!);
She welcomes him at home, as ever;
Elsewhere, a word or two will give;
At times, a bow she will award him;
At others, simply not regard him.
No spark of coquetry has she.
('Tis banned, in high society).
Onegin, ever paler growing,
She sees not – or she does not care?
He wastes, he dwindles in despair;
The symptoms of decline are showing.
The recommended quack says, 'Ah!
We doctors recommend the spa.'

32

But he stays put, busy preparing
A note to his forebears, to say
They soon shall meet. No cause for caring
Has Tanya. (Such is woman's way.)
Still he solicits her, persisting;
Hopes on and on, never desisting.
Sickness brings courage, to address
With feeble hand to his princess
A passionate communication.
Most letters have but small pretence,
He rightly thought, to point or sense;
Yet now, beyond all toleration
To anguish had his heart been stirred.
Hear now his letter, word for word: –

I well foresee how this confession
Of my sad secret will offend,
How your proud eyes will reprehend,
How bitter, scornful their expression.
What do I seek? What is my quest
In thus my inmost soul revealing?
Perhaps I cannot but suggest
Some joyful, some malicious feeling?

'We once met; it was accidental.
Your flash of tenderness so gentle
Seemed unbelievable to me.
My old sweet habits I rejected.
My freedom had to be protected,
My freedom, tedious though it be.
Another thing has come between us . . .

Lensky's sad death sets us apart . . .
From everything that could be seen as
Heartwarming I detached my heart;
An outcast, free from all restriction,
I thought in freedom to possess
A substitute for happiness.
What a mistake! What an infliction! . . .

'Not so: – to track you everywhere,
To mark your smiles, each movement noting;
To watch, with lover's eyes, where'er
Your eyes might fall; ever devoting
Long scrutiny, to comprehend
Your full perfection – yes, to perish,
Paling, in torments without end,
To cease: ah, that were bliss to cherish!

'But not for me! – for you, in vain
Here, everywhere, I trail and wander;
Each precious day, each hour must wane,
Whilst I, in fruitless tedium, squander
Those days, all numbered now by fate.
Too burdensome becomes their weight.
I know my life's of brief endurance;
To gain a longer span, I pray:
Give me each morning an assurance
That you and I shall meet that day.

'A small plea, but I can't help fearing
That your stern eyes therein may scan
Some cunning, despicable plan;
Your hot reproaches I keep hearing!
If you but knew the awful churning,
The anguished aching of my soul,
With only Mind to quell the burning,

The racing blood beyond control.
I long to clasp your knees, confessing,
Fall at your feet, sob with dismay,
Pour out my plaints and pleas, expressing
Every last thing a man could say.
Meanwhile I must appear phlegmatic,
My tongue and eyes well fortified.
My speech is calm, but, at your side,
Glancing at you, I feel ecstatic.

'So be it. I decline at last
To fight myself; my strength is slender.
I'm in your hands; the die is cast.
To destiny I now surrender.'

33

– No answer. Now behold him sending
Another letter – and one more.
No answer! Next, he is attending
A party; scarce within the door,
And – there is she . . . and how severely
She looks! She disregards him merely,
And speaks not. Ugh! he feels a cold,
Like January's, her enfold!
Those stubborn lips – what indignation
Are they not seeking to restrain?
He gazes fixedly – in vain
Seeks sympathy, or perturbation,
Or marks of tears . . . none, none! that face
Of naught but anger bears the trace.

34

Perhaps she fears herself in secret,
Lest to her husband she expose
– Or to the world – that slip, that weakness,
And all that my Onegin knows.
And now he drives away, despairing;
And, ever at his madness swearing,
Into its lowest deep is hurled,
And, once again, abjures the world;
Then, in his silent room, renewing
The past, remembers how the spleen
Through that same noisy world had been
Relentlessly his tracks pursuing,
And straightway by the collar took
And shut him in his gloomy nook.

35

Once more, he started random reading:
– Manzoni, Gibbon, and Rousseau;
Through Herder and De Staël proceeding,
And through Bichat, Chamfort, Tissot;
Read Bayle the sceptic's lucubrations,
Read all of Fontenelle's creations;
Some Russian author (please select!),
And nothing printed would reject:
Journals, or almanacks, repeating
Instructive precepts. Though they scold
Me now, it was not so of old;
They used to give me friendly greeting
With madrigals of praise; so, then,
È sempre bene, gentlemen!

36

His wrapt attention, though, was hollow;
His thoughts ranged far, beyond control.
Fanciful dreams, desire and sorrow
Were huddled deep within his soul.
Whilst on the printed lines he brooded,
Quite other lines and words intruded
Upon his spiritual eye,
And these engrossed him utterly: –
The dark mysterious traditions
Of days when hearts were warm and true;
And rumours, dreams without a clue,
And threatenings, and premonitions;
Gay, silly folktales, slow to end;
– Or letters, by a maiden penned.

37

A drowsy stupor now enfolds him;
Feeling and thought he disregards.
Mistress Imagination holds him,
Dealing her motley *faro* cards.
On soft snow – useless to deny it –
A young man lies, all still and quiet,
As if he has just gone to bed.
A voice is heard: 'That's it. He's dead.'
He sees old foes, calumniators,
Cowards, malignant; many a sworn
Comrade, whom now he holds in scorn;
A troop of women, young – all traitors!
Next, at a rural window, he
Beholds her sit – 'tis always She! . . .

38

Into this dreamy habit falling,
He very nearly lost his wit,
Or went the poet's way – a calling
So dire, don't even think of it!
And so, indeed, by power magnetic,
The nice machinery poetic
Of Russian verse he all but caught,
– This foolish fellow, whom I taught.
And, in a poet, how becoming
His air, when lost in his alcove,
He sat before the blazing stove,
And there, while *Benedetta* humming
Or purring *Idol mio* – *The News*
Dropt in the fire – or else his shoes.

39

The days sped by. Ere one could know it,
Winter dissolved in warmth. Though sad,
He did not make himself a poet,
Did not expire, did not go mad.
But rather, by the spring air quickened,
He left the close rooms where he'd sickened
And, marmot-like, slept winter through,
Left hearth and double-windows too,
One clear, bright morning, to go pelting
Sledge-borne along the Neva's shore.
On the blue, broken, icy floor
The sunshine plays; the snow is melting,
Uptorn and grimy, on the streets.
But whither now across it fleets

40

Onegin? – You have guessed, replying
Beforehand; as you apprehend,
To *her*, Tatyana, he is flying,
My strange, incorrigible friend.
He walks in, like some corpse decaying,
Encounters no-one on his way in,
Enters the next room – no-one there –
Opens a door . . . What meets his glare?
What stops him in his tracks, heart bleeding?
The princess – sitting in full sight,
Still in her *négligée*, all white,
With cheek on hand, alone and reading
Some kind of letter, it appears,
Her gentle face awash with tears.

41

Ah, but in that swift flash, who could not
Have fathomed all her dumb distress?
Who our poor, younger Tanya would not
Have recognized in that princess?
Yevgeny, full of ruth, in madness
Fell at her feet, o'erwrought with sadness;
She said no word, and shuddered, yet
Her gaze upon Onegin set
With no surprise, no indignation.
His ailing, his extinguished look,
Beseeching air, and dumb rebuke
She marked; like some reincarnation
Of that once simple maid she seems,
With her young heart, her early dreams.

42

She stares at him, her eyes not moving
From his; nor does she bid him stand;
Nor from his thirsty lips, reproving,
Withdraws her unresponsive hand.
What visions through her mind are thronging?
The silent pause no more prolonging,
At last she speaks, in tranquil tone: –
'Enough; now, rise; with you, I own,
There must be open explanation.
Onegin – I'll recall for you
When in the garden avenue
We met, by fate. Your exhortation
I heard, submissive then and dumb;
But now, today, my turn has come.

43

'I then, Onegin, they may tell me,
Was better: – younger, too, was I!
I loved you then; but what befell me?
And your heart gave me – what reply?
What found I in it? Rigour, purely!
A loving, humble girl was surely
No novelty to you? confess:
And now my blood just freezes, – yes,
Simply your icy look recalling,
And, heavens! that sermon that you gave . . .
Blameless, you managed to behave
With honour, in that hour appalling.
You acted right by me, I vow.
With all my soul, I thank you now.

44

'Is it not true that then, out yonder,
Far from the busy world's repute,
You liked me less as I grew fonder?
Then, why come now to persecute?
Why mark me down? Is this the reason, –
That I now figure, in due season,
In such high circles? That today
I'm rich and famous, as they say,
And have a husband maimed in fighting,
So that we are caressed at Court?
That all would notice and report
Any disgrace of my inciting?
That my disgrace is what you now seek –
And irresistible mystique?

45

'I weep now. But, if an abiding
Thought of your Tanya haunts you still
Know this: – your stinging words, your chiding
And your discourse, so stern, so chill,
Were better, could the choice be offered,
Than this insulting passion proffered,
Than all these letters, all these tears.
Then, you showed reverence for my years;
At least you had some pity for me,
For my young, girlish reverie:
But now! – what brings you here? I see
You kneeling at my feet, before me.
How can you, with your mind and heart,
Stoop to play this ignoble part?

46

'This pomp, which all in tinsel dresses
The life that I abhor so much;
My evenings, stylish house, successes
In the world's eddy – what are such
To me, Onegin? I'd surrender
Gladly, this minute, all the splendour,
Glitter and vapour, noise, parade
Of frippery in masquerade,
For our poor house . . . the garden by it
Left wild . . . that bookshelf; for the place
Where first I saw Onegin's face;
Ay, for that burial-ground so quiet,
Where my poor nurse reposes now
Beneath her cross and shadowing bough.

47

'Oh, happiness – we might have known it! . . .
We nearly did . . . Now destiny
Has sealed my fate; though – I must own it –
I may have acted foolishly.
My mother wept, adjured, besought me.
Poor Tanya! whatso fortune brought me,
To me was all the same; and so
I married. Now, I beg you, go;
Please leave me. Do as you are bidden.
I know your heart will be your guide
With all its honour and its pride.
I love you – can the truth be hidden? –
But now that I'm another's wife,
I shall stay faithful all my life.'

48

She left the room. Yevgeny, reeling,
Stands thunderstruck before the burst
Of tumult and tempestuous feeling
In which his heart is now immersed.
But what is this? – Spurs jingling gently,
Tatyana's husband makes his entry . . .
Acute embarrassment is nigh.
But here, my reader, you and I
Shall leave him, and our separation
Will last . . . for ever. Far have we
Proceeded in close company,
But that's enough. Congratulations –
We're home at last! Let's shout 'Hooray!' –
Not before time, I hear you say.

49

Dear reader, be you friend or foeman,
My feeling now is that we ought
To part in friendship and good omen.
Goodbye. Whate'er you may have sought
In reading through these trivial stanzas –
Memory's wild extravaganzas,
A change from work, impressive strokes,
Or silly little witty jokes,
Or, it may be, mistakes of grammar –
God grant within this book you find,
For fun, love or a dreamy mind
Or for the journalistic hammer,
Some crumb at least. Now you and I
Must go our separate ways. Goodbye.

50

And you, companion (of the oddest!),
Goodbye to you, my vision pure,
My vibrant, constant work – if modest.
Because of you I've held secure
All things that could delight a poet.
Flight from the stormy world? I know it.
Good conversation? That is mine.
Time speeds. It is a long, long time
Since Tanya, youthful and reflective,
And my Onegin next to her,
Came to me in a dreamy blur.
As to my novel's free perspective –
Hard though I scanned my crystal ball,
I could not make it out at all.

51

And what of those good friends who listened
To my first stanzas freshly made?
Some are no more and some are distant,
As Sadi said.[9] Without their aid
Onegin's portrait has been painted.
What of the girl who first acquainted
Me with Tatyana, perfect, pure? . . .
Fate's been a-thieving, to be sure . . .
Blest he who leaves a little early
Life's banquet without eating up
Or seeing the bottom of his cup,
Who drops his novel prematurely,
Bidding it suddenly adieu,
As I Yevgeny Onegin do.

THE END

NOTES

Chapter One

1 **baneful is the North to me . . . :** 'Written in Bessarabia' (Pushkin's note).

2 **Stanza 9** was discarded by Pushkin; also stanzas 13, 14, 39, 40 and 41.

3 ***bolivar:*** 'Hat *à la Bolivar*' (Pushkin's note).

4 ***Bréguet:*** A well-known watchmaker; a 'repeater' is meant.

5 ***Talon:*** 'A noted restaurant-keeper' (Pushkin's note).

6 **Applaud the capers of the ballet:** In the original, 'ready to clap an *entrechat*' – a dancing step.

7 **Fonvizin . . . Shakhovskoy: Fonvizin**, Denis Ivanovich, 1745–92: the notable writer of social and satiric comedies (*The Brigadier-General*, *The Minor*) in the age of Catherine II; also a translator, and a bold-spirited 'progressive' for his time. **Knyazhnin**, Yakov Borisovich, 1742–91, writer of comedies, also of tragedies (*Roslav*, *Vadim*). **Ozerov**, Vladislav Alexandrovich, 1770–1816, known for his 'classical' but sentimentalized tragedies (*Œdipus at Athens*, *Fingal*, and the patriotic *Dmitri of the Don*). **Semyonova**, Yekaterina Semyonovna, 1786–1849, a beautiful gifted actress, who played in Ozerov's and other classical tragedies, also in Shakespeare. **Katenin**, Pavel Alexandrovich, 1792–1853, a friend and appreciator of Pushkin, and a critic; he translated Racine and Marivaux as well as Corneille, and poems on 'old Russian life', in a national spirit; and had fought at Borodino and Leipzig. **Didelot**, Charles-Louis, 1767–1837, a founder of the Russian ballet and choreographer, who taught, e.g. Yevdokiya Il'inichna Istomina (*see* stanza 20), 1799–1848, whose beauty is said to have provoked more than one duel. **Shakhovskoy**, Alexander Alexandrovich, 1777–1846, a profuse writer of comedies and vaudevilles.

8 **Didelot:** 'A trait of refrigerated feeling, worthy of Childe Harold.

The ballets of G. Didelot are filled with lively imagination and extraordinary charm. One of our romantic writers found more poetry in them than in the whole of French literature' (Pushkin's note).

9 **Grimm:** Pushkin gives an extract from Rousseau's *Confessions* relating this incident, and adds: 'Grimm was before his age; today, throughout enlightened Europe, nails are cleaned with a special brush.'

10 **Dressed like Chadayev:** Lit., 'A second ***'; for the stars read Chadayev.

11 ***You,* first and foremost . . . without fail:** 'The Whole of this ironical stanza is nothing but a subtle eulogy of the lovely ladies, our contemporaries. It is thus that Boileau, under the veil of reproach, praises Louis XIV. Our ladies combine enlightenment with amiability, and strict purity of morals with that Oriental charm that so attracted Mme. de Staël' (Pushkin's note).

12 **The sky above the Neva's shore:** Pushkin here quotes at length 'a charming description of a Petersburg night from an idyll by Gnedich'.

13 **leaning on the granite, waited:** 'The enraptured poet – having hearkened to the kindly goddess – sees that he will pass a sleepless night – leaning on the granite (Muravyev, *To the Neva Goddess*)' (Pushkin's note).

14 **Tasso's octaves light:** *Ottava rima*, metre of Tasso's *Jerusalem Delivered*.

15 **O, Adriatic waters . . . haunt the sea:** 'Written at Odessa' (Pushkin's note) [1823–4].

16 **my own skies are African:** 'The author, on his mother's side, is of African descent. His great-grandfather, Abram Petrovich Hannibal, in his eighth year was kidnapped from the shores of Africa and carried to Constantinople. The Russian Ambassador rescued him and sent him as a present to Peter the Great, who stood his godfather in baptism at Vilna . . .' (From Pushkin's note).

17 **Ideal mountain-maiden sung:** In *The Prisoner of the Caucasus* and *The Fountain of Bakhchisaray*.

Chapter Two

1 **were consecrating . . .:** The rest of the stanza was discarded by Pushkin.

2 **Tatyana:** 'Sweet-sounding Greek names, for instance Agathon, Thilat, Thedora, Thekla, etc., are in use with us only among the common people' (Pushkin's note).

3 **Heaven's gift . . . happiness:** 'Si j'avois la folie de croire encore au bonheur, je le chercherois dans l'habitude (Chateaubriand)' (Pushkin's note).

4 **Shaved peasants' brows:** Recruits for the army had a lock shaved from their foreheads.

Chapter Three

1 **Let's go . . . in a jar:** Stanza imperfect in the original.

2 **(just like Svetlana):** Svetlana, heroine of the poem of that name, by Pushkin's friend Zhukovsky.

3 **Julie's favourite, Wolmar:** '*La Nouvelle Héloíse*. Malek-Adhel, hero of a mediocre romance by Mme. Cottin. Gustave de Linar, hero of a charming story by Baroness Krüdener' (Pushkin's note).

4 **The Vampire . . . Sbogar:** '*Vampire*, a tale wrongly attributed to Lord Byron. *Melmoth*, a production of genius by Maturin. Jean Sbogar, a well-known romance by Charles Nodier' (Pushkin's note). *The Vampire* (1819), by John William Polidori, was based on a sketch by Byron. *Melmoth the Wanderer* (1820), by Charles Robert Maturin, had much influence in France. Charles Nodier's tale *Jean Sbogar* appeared in 1818.

5 **the dame:** The professional matchmaker, who went between the families.

6 ***The Well-Disposed:*** The *Blagonamerenny*, a journal (1818–26), chiefly literary, conducted by A. E. Izmailov.

7 **Bogdanovich:** Ippolit Fyodorovich Bogdanovich (1743–1803), soldier and poet of the previous age, chiefly remembered for his story in verse, *Dushenka*.

8 **who singest:** 'E. A. Baratynsky' (Pushkin's note).

Chapter Four

1 **Stanzas 1–6** are lacking in the original.

2 **Tolstoy:** Fyodor Petrovich Tolstoy (1783–1873), the painter, sculp-

tor, medallion-maker and Hellenist, whose influence greatly raised the social status of artists in Russia.

3 **Baratynsky:** Yevgeny Abramovich Baratynsky (1800–44).

4 **Yazykov:** In a charming verse epistle of 14 June 1827 to Nikolay Mikhaylovich Yazykov (1803–46), Pushkin tells of their meeting long ago in Germany, when they drank together; laments Yazykov's debts and tells him not to pay them; let him, instead, feast and gamble, and cultivate Kypris – and Bacchus!

5 **The ode:** A retort by Pushkin to his friend Küchelbekker, who had urged in the journal *Mnemosyne* that 'elegies', and Pushkin's in particular, were a species inferior to the ode, which contained more 'rapture' (*vostorg*) and more poetry. In a prose note of 1824 Pushkin returns to the charge, saying that the ode is the lowest kind of poem, being destitute of 'plan', and that mere 'rapture' excludes the kind of 'tranquillity' (*spokoystviye*) which is 'an indispensable condition of the highest beauty' – a remark reminding one of a famous phrase by his contemporary, Wordsworth. 'Elegy', in the above stanzas, means any short meditative lyric, not necessarily melancholy.

6 **only festal odes . . . 'meaning strange':** *Chuzhoy Tolk*, a work of T. T. Dmitriev, in which he mocked at the ode. The 'artful lyric poet' is the pompous ode-maker.

7 **Breathe tragic speeches in some niche:** Morozov refers to Pushkin reading *Boris Godunov* aloud to his friend A. N. Wolff.

8 **Gulnare the fair:** Byron, *The Corsair*.

9 Rest of the stanza missing in the original; stanzas 36 and 37 were discarded.

10 **The maid:** 'Surprise has been expressed in the journals at it being possible to call a simple peasant girl *deva* [maiden], while gently-bred young ladies are called, a little later [Four, 28] *devchonki* [wenches]' (Pushkin's note).

11 **Pradt:** Dominique de Pradt (1759–1837), abbé, archbishop of Malines; ambassador at Warsaw; favoured by Napoleon, then royalist; publicist and copious writer.

12 **But, with its riotous foam . . . And for Aï:** Pushkin, in a note, quotes verses from *A Message to L. P.* 'In my fair years poetic Aï

pleased me with its noisy foam, with its likeness to love, to senseless youth', etc. – Aï, a small town in the present department of the Marne.

13 **La Fontaine's tales have shown it:** 'Auguste La Fontaine, author of a number of domestic romances' (Pushkin's note). Not the great Jean de La Fontaine, the fabulist.

Chapter Five

1 **Another bard, inspired divinely:** 'See *First Snow*, a poem by Prince Vyazemsky' (Pushkin's note).

2 **he can allure you . . . whose verse:** 'See the description of a Finnish winter in the *Eda* of Baratynsky' (Pushkin's note).

3 **The rings come out . . . A ditty:** Founded on a traditional 'under-dish' (*podblyudny*) carol and ceremony; the drawn rings signify 'fame', etc., for the lucky one ('the man', etc.).

4 **The maidens love the *tomcat* most:** '"The tom calls his puss to sleep, to the stove niche." A prediction of marriage; the first song presages death' (Pushkin's note).

5 ***Agathon*:** 'This is how they know the name of the future husband' (Pushkin's note).

6 **Svetlana:** See Chapter Two, note 2.

7 **Lel:** a god of love and marriage, in old Slavonic legend.

8 **Yevgeny sways her:** 'One of our critics apparently finds in these lines an impropriety, to us unintelligible' (Pushkin's note).

9 **Martin Zadeck:** 'Books of fortune-telling are published in Russia by the firm of Martin Zadeck, an estimable man, who never wrote any books of fortune-telling . . .' (Pushkin's note).

10 **Malvina:** A romance (1816–18) by Mme. Cottin.

11 **epics (two) on Peter:** One of these *Petriads* was a heroic poem in ten cantos (1817) by Alexander Gruzintsev.

12 **Dawn, with her purple finger:** 'A parody of Lomonosov's well-known lines, "The morn with purple finger From the quiet morning waters Comes out, with the sun behind her", etc.' (Pushkin's note).

13 **Buyanov:** Pushkin, in a note, quotes from a poem, *The Dangerous*

Neighbour, a description of one Buyanov, unshaven, in peaked cap, etc. He was a 'cousin' in the sense of being the hero of this poem by Pushkin's uncle, V. L. Pushkin. See stanza 44.

14 **wenches:** 'Our critics, true respecters of the fair sex, have severely condemned the indecorum of this stanza' (Pushkin's note). See note 8 above.

15 **Zizi:** A familiar name of Pushkin's for Yevpraksiya N. Wolff, sister of his friend A. N. Wolff.

16 Pushkin discarded stanzas 37, 38, also 43 below.

17 **Alban:** Francesco Albani (1578–1660), an Italian painter of mythological subjects.

18 **My cousin, then – he's somewhat heady:** See note 13 above.

Chapter Six

1 **Verrey:** 'A Parisian restaurant-keeper' (Pushkin's note).

2 **Public opinion, too, behold it!:** 'A line of Griboyedov' (Pushkin's note).

3 15, 16, were discarded stanzas.

4 **Lepage:** 'A famous gunsmith' (Pushkin's note).

5 Discarded by Pushkin.

6 **motley shoes:** The bast shoe of the peasant, *lapot'*.

Chapter Seven

1 **You run down Moscow? . . . none of us:** From Sir Bernard Pares's translation of *Gore ot Uma*.

2 **Levshin:** 'Levshin, author of many works on domestic economy' (Pushkin's note).

3 8, 9, discarded by Pushkin.

4 **A statuette . . . tight-crossed arms:** An image of Napoleon.

5 **Our roads are now abominable:** Pushkin, in a note, quotes twenty lines from a poem by Vyazemsky, *The Station*, in which, while praising the sward, etc., by the roads ('a garden for the eye'), he deplores their

badness, saying that they are icebound in winter, while in summer there is a sultry drought; and he wishes that Russia had a *McAdam* [J. L. McAdam, 1756–1836] to make them.

6 **The mile-posts flash, like palings, by:** 'The comparison is borrowed from K—, known for his lively imagination; K— relates how once, when he was sent as a courier from Prince Potemkin to the Empress, he rode so fast that his sword, the end of which hung out of the telega, rattled along the verst-posts as if they were a paling' (Pushkin's note).

7 **Now, Peter's fort . . . lions topping gates:** 'On the former English Club, now the Museum of the Revolution, on Tverskaya' (N. L. Brodsky, *Yevgeny Onegin: Roman A. S. Pushkina*, Moscow, 1932).

8 Discarded.

9 **Kharitonye:** Near St Khariton's Church, in the parish of St Khariton.

10 **St Simeon:** Church of St Simeon Stylites.

11 **she:** Thought to refer to Alexandra Korsakova (Brodsky's *Commentary*: see note 7 above).

Chapter Eight

1 Stanza unfinished in the original. In 1815, Pushkin, at a ceremony in the Tsarskoe Selo Lyceum, read some verses to the old poet G. A. Derzhavin (1743–1816).

2 **rout:** '*Rout*, an evening assembly without any dances, properly signifies a crowd' (Pushkin's note).

3 **my own Demon:** His lines, *The Demon*, written in 1823; – in his days of youth, joy, and aspiration, the poet is visited by a malicious Genius, who poisons his heart, whispers that all is illusion, and pours scorn on the ideals of love and freedom.

4 **Chatsky:** The hero Alexander Griboyedov's comedy *Gore ot Uma* (*The Mischief of Being Clever*), 1824.

5 **(– sorry, Shishkov):** Admiral A. S. Shishkov, known for his dislike of imported foreign words.

6 **Not that I . . . :** i.e. 'can help using the word'.

7 Stanza imperfect in the original.

8 **The sisters' monogram:** Referring to a court distinction, resembling that of a Maid of Honour or Lady-in-Waiting, which entitled the holder, a *Freylina* (Fräulein), to wear a decoration with initials.

9 **Sadi:** The great Persian poet (thirteenth century).

PUSHKIN AND HIS CRITICS

Vladimir Nabokov defines and describes the text of *Yevgeny Onegin* in the Introduction to his literal translation of the novel.

> The novel is mainly concerned with the emotions, meditations, acts, and destinies of three men: Onegin, the bored fop; Lenski, the minor elegiast; and a stylized Pushkin, Onegin's friend. There are three heroines: Tatiana, Olga, and Pushkin's Muse. Its events are placed between the end of 1819, in St Petersburg (Chapter One), and the spring of 1825, in St Petersburg again (Chapter Eight). The scene shifts from the capital to the countryside, midway between Opochka and Moscow (Chapter Two to the beginning of Seven), and thence to Moscow (end of Seven). The appended passages from *Onegin's Journey* (which were to be placed between Chapters Seven and Eight) take us to Moscow, Novgorod, the Volga region, the Caucasus, the Crimea, and Odessa.
>
> The themes and structural devices of Eight echo those of One. Each chapter has at least one peacock spot: a young rake's day in One (15–36), the doomed young poet in Two (6–38), Tatiana's passion for Onegin in Three, rural and literary matters in Four, a fatidic nightmare and a name-day party in Five, a duel in Six, a journey to Moscow in Seven, and Onegin's passion for Tatiana in Eight. Throughout there is a variety of romantic, satirical, biographical, and bibliographical digressions that lend the poem wonderful depth and color. In my notes I have drawn the reader's attention to the marvellous way Pushkin handles certain thematic items and rhythms such as the 'overtaking-and-hanging-back' device (One), interstrophic enjambments (Tatiana's flight into the park and Onegin's ride to Princess N.'s house), and the little leitmotiv of a certain phrase running through the entire novel. Unless these and other mechanisms and every other detail of the text are consciously assimilated, *EO* cannot be said to exist in the reader's mind.
>
> Pushkin's composition is first of all and above all a phenomenon of style, and it is from this flowered rim that I have surveyed its sweep of Arcadian country, the serpentine gleam of its imported

> brooks, the miniature blizzards imprisoned in round crystal, and the many-hued levels of literary parody blending in the melting distance. It is not 'a picture of Russian life'; it is at best the picture of a little group of Russians, in the second decade of the last century, crossed with all the more obvious characters of western European romance and placed in a stylized Russia, which would disintegrate at once if the French props were removed and if the French impersonators of English and German writers stopped prompting the Russian-speaking heroes and heroines. The paradoxical part, from a translator's point of view, is that the only Russian element of importance is this speech, Pushkin's language, undulating and flashing through verse melodies the likes of which had never been known before in Russia.

From the introduction, *Eugene Onegin*, transl. Vladimir Nabokov, vol. I, Bollingen series LXXII, Pantheon Books, 1964, pp. 6–8.

Nabokov goes on to describe the 'Onegin' stanza. (In doing so he ignores the tradition of using capital letters for feminine (two-syllable) rhymes and lower-case letters for masculine (one-syllable) ones. His preference is to indicate feminine rhymes by vowels and masculine ones by consonants. Thus the 'Onegin' stanza, with a rhyme-scheme normally described as AbAbCCddEffEgg, appears in his version as ababeecciddiff).

> The *EO* stanza, as a distinct form, is Pushkin's invention (9 May 1823). It contains 118 syllables and consists of fourteen lines, in iambic tetrameter, with a regular scheme of feminine and masculine rhymes: ababeecciddiff. The abab part and the ff part are usually very conspicuous in the meaning, melody, and intonation of any given stanza. This opening pattern (a clean-cut sonorous elegiac quatrain) and the terminal one (a couplet resembling the code of an octave or that of a Shakespearean sonnet) can be compared to patterns on a painted ball or top that are visible at the beginning and at the end of the spin. The main spinning process involves eecciddi, where a fluent and variable phrasing blurs the contours of the lines so that they are seldom seen as clearly consisting of two couplets and a closed quatrain. The iddiff part is more or less distinctly seen as consisting of two tercets in only one third of the entire number of stanzas in the eight cantos, but even in these cases the closing couplet often stands out so prominently as to cause the Italian form to intergrade with the English one.

From the introduction, *Eugene Onegin*, transl. Vladimir Nabokov, vol. I, Bollingen series LXXII, Pantheon Books, 1964, p. 10.

John Bayley also considers the effect of the 'Onegin' stanza, preceding these remarks by a discussion of Pushkin's claim to have written a 'novel in verse'.

> *Evgeny Onegin* is a triumphant hybrid; the most glitteringly poetic of poems, and yet as full of 'felt life' as the most richly conceived work of fiction. Before examining how it works, and analysing one of its chapters in detail, it is worth looking for a moment at the idea of the verse novel, and its relation during the nineteenth century to the novel in prose. In his essay 'Is Verse a Dying Technique?' Edmund Wilson suggested that Flaubert, Joyce and Virginia Woolf were in a sense poets who wrote in prose because at the time they were writing only a prose form seemed to offer the freedom and the authority for the kinds of fictional experiment they wished to attempt. Such novels resemble the kind of poetry which keeps our attention fixed on its medium, and embodies in its physical identity what it says and the nature of the world it creates. By contrast the evolved realistic prose novel takes its medium for granted in the interest of its exposition and narrative viewpoint – the authority of the novelist as a 'man speaking to men' both assumes and overrides the mode of presentation. The 'poetic novel', on this showing, is at least as old as *Tristram Shandy*, which, as we shall see, is more closely related to the form of *Evgeny Onegin* than is the more obvious parallel of Byron's *Don Juan*.
>
> The significant kinship of the novel in verse is thus with new kinds of novel in prose, rather than with traditional long poems. And the comparative failure of most verse novels of the nineteenth century is usually due to the author's inability to rid himself of the instinctive assumption that he is writing a long poem. The epic or narrative poem cannot by nature easily adopt the relative form. Arms and the man it sings, or man's first disobedience, or the growth of a poet's mind; and for all the ingenuity of its composite and relative presentation, Browning's *The Ring and the Book* is really as straightforwardly didactic as Wordsworth's *Excursion*, Cowper's *Task* or Crabbe's *Borough* . . .
>
> The medium of *Evgeny Onegin* as in their differing ways those of *Tristram Shandy*, *Dead Souls*, *Don Juan*, *Finnegans Wake* or *The Waves* – is continually brought to our notice by the author: Byron and Pushkin lay it before us in the repetition of every fresh stanza, and we may note that the most successful verse novels employ a highly idiosyncratic and demanding stanza form. The

impression is one of constant and brilliant improvisation, problems and contingencies recurring in endless permutation, and being solved and disposed of with an ever renewed cunning, labour, and expertise, which masks itself (particularly in the case of Byron) under the guise of a dazzling helplessness. The author is far too busy to be detached and authoritative: he cannot be expected to *know*, for he escapes at every moment into the new patterns of the structure he is creating. Hence the relative viewpoint is really built into the exigence of such a work, and is virtually the consequence of each fresh and yet ever recurrent crisis, compromise, and solution.

The form of Pushkin's stanza lends itself perfectly to this process. Its regularity holds endless permutations of tone, stress, and flow; and yet at the same time the unchanging metrical coordinates of its fourteen lines, rhyming *ababeecciddiff*, lead us with each verse to new contemplation and appraisal of what it achieves. *Ruslan and Lyudmila* is a traditional narrative poem in that the freely rhymed paragraphs eventually distract the reader – as with couplets or blank verse or the prose of an ordinary novel – from this kind of renewed awareness: he falls in with the medium and begins to take it for granted as he concentrates on the tale. Pushkin seems to have hit on his new stanza form by regularising a more or less chance arrangement that occurs not infrequently in the *contes* of La Fontaine, from which Pushkin, like other Russian poets before him (Dimitriev was one) had derived the irregularly rhyming tetrameter measure of their narrative poems . . .

The parallel with the sonnet sequence is instructive; and it is tempting to suggest that the fascination and dramatic elusiveness of Shakespeare's Sonnets, which have provoked so many inadequately schematic and 'non-relative' interpretations, are also the logical result of a medium comparably handled. The poet appears to commit himself, plays with that appearance, withdraws, modifies his approach, introduces and repeats with variations another theme; again reveals himself, and again compounds the revelation with a change of tone and the introduction of a further set of variations. The process lends itself to a seeming irresponsibility which is both justified and transfigured by the verbal dexterity and psychological adroitness of the poet. When we think we have him we find he is no longer there, and his words open out an ambiguous glitter of perspective . . .

From John Bayley, *Pushkin: a Comparative Commentary*, Cambridge University Press, 1971, pp. 236–8.

Bayley goes on to consider the complex tone of the novel and suggests that it is bewitched by the spirit of parody.

> The complex tone of the novel is kept in continual balance between objectivity and confiding personal engagement. Each has its sphere precisely allotted, and the many cancelled stanzas almost always reflect a temporary loss of balance or a collision between the two, for the dramatic relation of characters is seldom directly exposed to what is known to Pushkin only – his personal interventions do not directly impinge on them. This again is an aspect of the novel in poetry, whose unique form makes it possible. The eighteenth-century novelists whom Pushkin depends on most – Sterne, Richardson, Rousseau – and in whose climate *Evgeny Onegin* began to live and take shape, offer no corresponding contrast between the objective tale and the authorial presence.
>
> In them the consciousness of the writer is the world of the novel. Rousseau's claim to uniqueness and to the possession of an individuality 'such as no one else has had since the creation of the world', acted as an intoxicant upon the reader of fiction, and the writer of it. Everyone perceived instantly how to be unique, and the result was the immense crop of imitations which followed the appearance of *Clarissa* and *Sir Charles Grandison*, *La Nouvelle Héloïse* and *The Sentimental Journey*. A new standardisation of personal feeling succeeded the revelation of its individuality. Sterne's sentiment could be imitated, and was imitated in Russia by Radishchev and Karamzin, and the gloom of young Werther and the sensibility of Julie de Wolmar had their echoes in Russia as in the rest of Europe. But by breaking the form Pushkin was able to escape the new conventions that had risen out of imitation. The sentimental novel of love and death appears in a wholly different light when told in glittering octosyllabics, and the poet accentuates the discrepancy by himself standing back, and withdrawing his sensibility from the scene which it should have dominated. As a sentimental novel *Evgeny Onegin* is like nature without God, and Pushkin, the *deus absconditus*, turns the subjective sensibility into an objective property, ornament, and plaything.
>
> As we shall see, the formalist critic Shklovsky, in a brilliant critique of *Evgeny Onegin*, demonstrates the ways in which it parodies the novel, the novel of sentiment in particular, and we shall return to discuss his findings. The question and quality of parody is never far away in Pushkin, and his novel in verse is bewitched by it. But it never appears schematic – ivory box arranged inside ivory box . . . The depth of the thing, as usual with Pushkin, is in the contrasts and confrontations which its

artificiality makes possible. Even the most ingenious parodist is apt to be oblivious of the plain reality which involuntarily enters his fiction – chairs, typewriters, dirty glasses, ashtrays – while he concentrates on its point. Pushkin appears to take note of and describe these things at the same moment that he imitates a fellow-poet, plays variations on a sentimental landscape theme, or creates his heroine's consciousness in terms of the heroes and heroines she has read about in books. His characters, no less than himself, are surrounded by the mundane and unchanging facts and relations of life, and these are in the novel, along with every sort of literary and stylistic attitude towards them.

From John Bayley, *Pushkin: a Comparative Commentary*, Cambridge University Press, 1971, pp. 244–5.

J. Douglas Clayton provides a definition of Yevgeny Onegin as a 'catalogue of negatives', showing that he existed outside the expected codes of career and behaviour.

The notion of 'type' very quickly begins to break down when subjected to closer scrutiny – is it, to put it simply, the lowest common denominator or the highest common factor of the generation? Is a typical character ordinary, the statistical average, or is he exaggerated, a caricature possessing the 'typical' qualities of the age to an extreme degree? Even if we have accepted the latter proposition, we have simply moved the question a step back, for now it must be asked what the 'typical' qualities are, and how they are determined. Even a cursory glance at such figures as Oblomov and Bazarov suggests that, whatever their authors and audience thought they were, they are interesting not because they resemble their contemporaries but because they are different . . .

What I intend to dispute in the following pages is the notion that Onegin was a normal young man who was somehow representative of his age (which is what I take the word 'type' to mean). Even the foreword that was placed before Chapter One when it was first printed, if read carefully, does not bear out such an assumption: 'The first chapter is in a way a whole. It contains the description of the life of a young man in Petersburg society at the end of 1819'. Pushkin's statement is laconic, yet specific: we are to read the description of the life of a certain young man at a certain place at a certain time. The conclusions are left for the reader to draw for himself. No notion of typicality is imposed.

This is not surprising, since if we examine Onegin closely we find that, far from being the representative of his age, he is a very unusual individual, and that he is defined, not in terms of what he is, but rather in terms of what he is not, or more precisely, in terms of the activities that he avoids. Onegin has to be seen, that is to say, against the background of his age, an age that ascribed very clear roles to individuals . . .

In the notional world of *Onegin*, a particularly important choice is that between service and non-service. All three principals, Onegin, Lenskii, and Pushkin, have essentially chosen the path of non-service. In the case of Pushkin, true, the poet was 'officially' a functionary in the Ministry (Collegium) of Foreign Affairs. In fact this was purely a matter of form and does not play any role in the work . . . although service (either military or civil) to the state was no longer absolutely obligatory, as it had been under Peter the Great, it was the normal path for the vast majority of Onegin's contemporaries . . . Onegin's non-service is thus not simply a chance feature of his biography but a highly significant trait which underlines Onegin's egoism and indifference to Russia, and it is made even more heinous by his cult of Napoleon, manifested by the presence of the French emperor's statuette in his study (discovered by Tat'iana in Chapter Seven). (In this context it should be noted that both Pushkin and Lenskii were too young to serve in the Napoleonic wars, and that their non-service is caused by their decision to undertake the life of a poet.)

The second kind of choice that Onegin appears to have made is in the category 'Decembrist/non-Decembrist'. The Decembrist movement (as it became known after its tragic dénouement on the Senate Square in Petersburg on 14 December 1825) was an underground movement of young officers who became inflamed with revolutionary ideas while serving in Europe during the Napoleonic wars and formed secret societies dedicated to the overthrow of the Tsarist régime and the abolition of serfdom in Russia. Pushkin himself was on the fringes of the movement, but was saved, paradoxically enough, from the dire consequences of involvement in the events of December by the fact that he was in exile on his family's estate of Mikhailovskoe for earlier misdeeds . . .

There is, needless to say, very little in the way of Decembrism to be wrung out of Onegin's thoughts on political economy. Far from being an idealistic revolutionary concerned with the fate of his country, Onegin is, like his father, a thoughtless spendthrift who squanders his patrimony and whose 'new order' on the estate he has inherited from his uncle reflects not a humanitarian concern for the serf but a lack of regard for his own financial interests, which he is willing to sacrifice to a whim, or at best to the desire to be in fashion. The reaction of the serfs is characteristic: 'the slave blessed his fate' – implying that the actions of the young lord are as incomprehensible to him as the turns of destiny, and that no thanks are required for such an act of folly. Pushkin, it seems to me, is ironical about rather than approving of Onegin's gesture, which is made, he suggests, out of boredom and is another manifestation of his insouciant nature.

Perhaps the most convincing argument about Onegin's 'un-Decembrist' nature is the reaction of the Decembrist writers themselves (principally Ryleev and Bestuzhev), who were dismayed at the Onegin whom they saw in Chapter One . . . Instead of finding in *Onegin* a virtuous, idealistic, and self-sacrificing hero to be emulated, the Decembrists were shocked by the frivolity, selfishness, and cynicism of Onegin's life-style . . . It is therefore straining credulity to see in Onegin an attempt, either overt or covert, to portray a Decembrist. Neither his life-style of indolence, debauchery, and self-indulgence, nor his cynical and egoistic opinions nor his boredom and spleen correspond to the codes of behaviour and the literary norms which 'read' as Decembrist. His act of munificence – freeing his serfs from their corvée – is the arbitrary act of an 'eccentric' (*chudak* – which is what his neighbours call him) who is uncaring of his own fate and fortune and who feels no urge to preserve his patrimony for posterity.

Onegin, then, far from being a 'type', is outside all the accepted career/behaviour codes – a non-military, non-functionary non-Decembrist. For the purposes of the novel, however, there is a fourth 'negative' which we have to add, and one which, in the context of *Onegin*, is of paramount importance. He is not a poet . . . The detail is important since the other two principal characters – Lenskii and Pushkin – are poets, and because [. . .] the notion of 'being a poet' has important existential connotations in the work. What we are talking about here, however, is less these than the simple question of a function, a career, a role that gives one a place in society and gives meaning to one's existence . . .

Onegin as 'non-poet' has, however, another dimension that should be mentioned, namely the fact that he cannot tell an iambus (– /) from a choree (/ –). The reason is apparently that Onegin is largely a French-speaker who has read only French poetry and for whom the notion of stress as a significant feature in metre is foreign and incomprehensible. It is made clear to the reader that the correspondence between Tat'iana and Onegin is likewise in French (Three, 26), as, given the norms of social behaviour of the time, would be the conversations as well. It was, indeed, quite practical even for a young nobleman of the time to function knowing hardly any Russian (as did A. N. Raevskii, a friend of Pushkin's whom some chose to see as the 'prototype' on whom Pushkin modelled his hero). We are told that Onegin communicates to his neighbours without putting the polite enclitic *-s* when replying *da* and *net*. One suspects that these monosyllables constitute the largest part of his conversation, so that if Lenskii, despite his Russian elegies, is described by his neighbours as 'half-Russian' (Two, 5, 12), then it would be legitimate to call Onegin 'non-Russian'.

Onegin, then, is a catalogue of negatives, a 'dangerous eccentric' who appears as the personification of the 'spirit of denial' . . .

From J. Douglas Clayton, *Ice and Flame*, University of Toronto Press, 1985, pp. 139–45.

By contrast, William Mills Todd discusses the complexity of contemporary conventions and the attitude towards them shown by Pushkin and his characters. He goes on to consider one of the urgent aesthetic questions of that time – the nature and responsibility of literature.

Conventions assume many guises in *Eugene Onegin*: norms and rules; fashions which bear arbitrary temporal limits of applicability; and customs, which have greater permanence. At times they are the property of different social groups. Conventions, basically, are repeated actions which enable members of a group (with or without having to think about it) to define situations, to predict the results of their actions, and to understand the actions of others by a process of decoding and anticipation. Conventions allow Eugene with his fashionable haircut, perfect French, and unforced manner of talking – scant information, indeed, but essential to the *honnête homme* – to be accepted in high society as 'intelligent and very nice'(One, 4). When, on the other hand, he refuses to meet with his rural neighbors, use the particles of their polite speech, and kiss their wives' hands, his behavior corresponds to none of their conventional expectations, and, in their anxiety, they imagine him an ignoramus, a madman, or a 'Farmazon' (illiterate rendering of 'Freemason', Two, 5), since only these types would so ignore the conventions which hold society together. But merely by appearing at the home of an unmarried girl, he reintegrates himself into their conventional expectations and can be inserted, inaccurately it turns out, into the role of a suitor. Meanwhile, Tatiana, who also ignores social conventions, but whose understanding of life is shaped by literary ones, views this silent newcomer as a hero like those in her sentimentalist novels and acts upon this assumption.

Eugene Onegin presents no simple attitude toward conventions because there are so many ways of observing and not observing them, and because different ones (literary and social, for example) may have relevance to the same situation. One may observe conventions in a blindly childish fashion (Lensky, Tatiana initially), with resignation (the narrator giving us an expected rhyme), or with creative energy. Indeed, many of the most elegant passages in the novel, those expressing the poet's longing for Venice (One, 48–9) and his love of pastoral pleasures (One, 55), for example, echo familiar traditions of Western literature.

Disrespect for conventions in *Eugene Onegin* covers a similarly broad range of possibilities, from the creative mixing of genres (a novel in verse) to the fashionable and socially acceptable eccentricity of Eugene (an accomplished dandy) to insultingly casual disregard (Eugene's use of his valet as his second in the duel) to potentially dangerous violation (Tatiana's letter to Eugene).

Clearly these attitudes toward conventionality can be translated into understanding or action with varying degrees of success, depending on the knowledge and intelligence of the characters, author and reader who use them . . .

Perhaps the conventions which *Eugene Onegin* most persistently offers for examination are those which relate literary and social facets of culture. Here, consequently, one encounters central aesthetic problems of Pushkin's time: the nature and responsibility of literature. Should literature as an institution use language in a *referential* fashion – representing reality according to some standard of verisimilitude? Or *emotive* – expressing the poet's feelings and attitudes? Or *conative* – supplicating and exhorting the reader, issuing moral imperatives? Among Pushkin's contemporary readers and critics one finds reproaches on all of these grounds: *Eugene Onegin* has represented reality in an improper or insufficient manner . . .; *Eugene Onegin* devotes too much space to the author-narrator or has too much borrowed material, the tone is Byron's, not Pushkin's . . .; *Eugene Onegin* lacks moral seriousness . . . Or, finally, could literature be language in its *aesthetic* function, language which calls attention to itself as an aesthetic object divorced from instrumental functions? Perhaps the tersest expression of this formalistic attitude in Western literature was issued by Pushkin himself in a polemical note to Zhukovsky: 'The goal of poetry is poetry'.

From William Mills Todd III, *Fiction and Society in the Age of Pushkin: Ideology, Institutions, and Narrative*, Harvard University Press, 1986, pp. 125–7.

Richard Freeborn gives us his view of Tatyana at the end of the story, emphasising her strong moral awareness and the way in which the final scene of the novel would serve as a model for future Russian writers.

> Although surrounded in St Petersburg by the social throng, Tatyana remains as ever a solitary, temperamentally remote from the *beau monde* as she is morally above it. Her reaction therefore to Onegin's love for her, sympathetic and understanding though it may be, is tinged with anger (Eight, 33). He demeans himself in her eyes by such a display of passion for her. In their last encounter the most pointed of the things she says – and this is the only time she speaks to Onegin, so far as we know, during the entire work – is contained in the rhetorical assertion that her shame in succumbing to his advances would surely be noticed by all and would lend Onegin a certain alluring esteem in the eyes of society. How can he, a man of such heart and intellect, be slave to such a shallow feeling? (Eight, 44, 45)
>
> What she appeals to in him, and what she upholds in herself, is a morality that transcends convention. Her final words are a statement of her moral duty, in that Fate has ordained she should be given to another, to whom she will be faithful for the rest of her life. The triteness of these sentiments should not be allowed to obscure the declaration of private morality which the words clearly express. It has to be assumed that Tatyana is the touchstone of true moral good sense by which the moral worth of the hero is to be judged. Both may be caught in the toils of that Fate which is reality itself, or so Belinsky would have us believe, surrounding both hero and heroine like the air they breathe, but what is most real in terms of human experience in the whole of *Eugene Onegin* is this moment when Tatyana, though she loves him deeply, feels in duty bound to reject Onegin's love for her and all possibility of their mutual happiness . . .
>
> The final scene of the meeting between Onegin and Tatyana has a psychological and dramatic profundity which is to serve as a model for all future developments in the Russian novel. Relying little in construction on coincidence or plot, the Russian novel, in its greatest examples, is a form designed to enact a situation, a particular scene, a present dramatic immediacy in which the lives and spirits of human beings are suddenly penetrated, illuminated and laid bare. Pechorin's discovery of himself, Chichikov's ultimate discomfiture, the meaning of Oblomov's dream, Raskolnikov's disenchantment, Andrey Bolkonsky's knowledge of love in death, Pierre Bezukhov's discovery of God in life are all offered to us as moments of revelation when the meaning of each life is

dramatically illuminated. The history of the evolution of the Russian nineteenth-century novel may be seen as an ever deeper penetration into the privacy of human experience or an ever greater intrusion into the intimacies of private rooms. There is always a clear opposition between public and private areas of experience, but there is also an equally clear assumption that, though the areas interpenetrate, the public facade requires to be known before the private life can be revealed. In each case the private dilemma mirrors the divisiveness of society; in each case it asserts its independence of social causes. We leave Onegin at the moment when his irrelevance to society is a great deal less real to him than his irrelevance to Tatyana; whether or not he is superfluous in social terms matters less than his private failure to transcend the conventional *comme il faut* of the St Petersburg world where he and Tatyana confront each other as equals. What Tatyana asserts – and what other heroes and heroines of the Russian novel will assert – is the privacy of conscience, the singularity of all moral awareness and certitude, the discovery of the single, unique moral self which opposes and withstands the factitious morality of the mass, of society, humanity or the general good.

From Richard Freeborn, *The Rise of the Russian Novel*, Cambridge University Press, 1973, pp. 35–7.

Prince Dmitri Mirsky presents an assessment of the novel from the viewpoint of an educated Russian. Describing it as a 'living growth', he discusses its provenance, the exquisite poetry of the first chapter, Pushkin's 'method of character drawing', the power of his poetry to command obedience through fascination and the need to see *Yevgeny Onegin* as the fullest expression of the poet's early lyrical and subjective manner.

Evgeni Onegin is like a living growth: the same throughout, and yet different. We recognize in the eighth chapter the style of the first as we recognize a familiar face, changed by age. The difference is great and yet the essential proportions are the same. It is a face of unique beauty.

The genealogy of Pushkin's manner in *Evgeni Onegin* is complicated and includes many foreign ancestors. The initial French groundwork is always recognizable. It is thoroughly Russian, so Russian as even to be incapable of reproduction in any other tongue. But it is the Russian of an age that spoke French as well as and oftener than Russian. Pushkin never disclaimed this French flavour of his Russian. He alludes to it often, humorously and affectionately. He does not omit to mention, before quoting it, that Tatiana's letter to Onegin was written in French, and that his translation of the 'original' is only 'the pale copy of a living picture' . . .

Byron and Sterne are other 'sources' of the *Onegin* manner. But they were stimulants, first suggestions of great possibilities, and nothing more. After all, the manner is neither French, nor Byronic, nor Sternian, but Russian and Pushkinian – and perhaps the most original, personal, and freeborn of all Pushkin's manners. Its magic lightfootedness is as unlike the laboured and premeditated conceits of *Tristram Shandy*, as it is unlike the somewhat slovenly ease of *Don Juan*. This lightness of touch, the most unique and inimitable thing in the *Onegin* manner, persists throughout the novel and links the otherwise so different first and eighth chapters into one whole.

But the triumph, the pure quintessence of the style, is in the first chapter. Here it reaches its greatest freedom and expansive force. It bubbles and plays like a fountain in the sun. Its sparkling lightness has been compared to a newly uncorked champagne bottle, and its exhilarating effect can be likened to nothing but champagne. The lyrical digressions especially, so spontaneous, so effortless, so divinely light, give that effect of creation out of the void which is not elsewhere to be found in Pushkin. The flawless perfection of the craftsmanship is all the more striking as it is quite concealed and can produce nothing but the effect of absolutely spontaneous improvisation on the lay reader. The youthful exuberance of this first unfettered flight is somewhat sobered down in the later chapters. But the essential lightness and spontaneity of the style remains. The story is told spaciously and freely. It moves in an atmosphere of pure yet earthly and unromantic poetry, where humour and feeling form a blend of exquisite mellowness . . .

The characters of Onegin and Tatiana have been so profusely written about that it is as difficult to tackle the subject as it is to taste food that has been in many mouths . . . I must ask leave to refrain from discussing the subject.

What has been given less attention is Pushkin's method of character drawing. It is different from his own method in his plays and novels, and still more different from that of his narrative poems (where the characters are only geometrical knots of situations). The characters of *Evgeni Onegin* are the least classical productions of Pushkin's workshop. They are very largely achieved by 'suggestion' and 'atmosphere'. They are essentially lyrical. They are irreducibly individual, but this individuality of theirs is not achieved by the objective methods of Tolstoy,

Dostoyevsky, or Proust, not by the actions or words that are ascribed to them, but by what the poet himself says of them and by the way he says it. Their unity is one of atmosphere, and in this respect it is again Turgenev who is the truest disciple of Pushkin (or rather of the author of *Onegin*). It is essentially irrelevant to look for psychological consistency in the personalities of Onegin or of Tatiana, for their portraits are not achieved by objective psychological methods. Contemporary criticism, for instance, not without good grounds noticed an inconsistency between the Tatiana of the eighth and of the previous chapters. We do not, as a rule, remark this, however familiar we may be with the poem, and even the more familiar we are the less we see the inconsistency. Our Tatiana is the rural Tatiana of the early chapters plus the married Tatiana, and we see each half-Tatiana in terms of the whole Tatiana. Still, psychologically and logically speaking, the gulf between the two is very real, and it is bridged by no psychological bridgework, only by a poet's arbitrary *sic iubeo*. We have obeyed the poet, but we have done so because we have been fascinated by his lyrical power, not because we have weighed the objective evidence as we have been allowed to do in the case of a very similar transformation, that of Tolstoy's Natasha. In this sense *Evgeni Onegin* is evidently lyrical and subjective and . . . it is the ripest and fullest expression of Pushkin's early, lyrical, and subjective manner.

From Prince D. S. Mirsky, *Pushkin*, George Routledge & Sons, 1926, pp. 147–50.

SUGGESTIONS FOR FURTHER READING

Much detailed information about *Yevgeny Onegin* is to be found in the commentary (vols 2 and 3) to Vladimir Nabokov, *'Eugene Onegin': Translation and Commentary*, 4 vols, Bollingen Foundation, New York, 1964.

The following books are devoted to this work alone:

A. D. P. Briggs, *Eugene Onegin*, Landmarks of World Literature, Cambridge, 1992.

D. Chizhevsky, *Evgenij Onegin*, Cambridge, Mass., 1953.

J. D. Clayton, *Ice and Flame: Pushkin's 'Eugene Onegin'*, Toronto, 1985.

S. S. Hoisington, *Russian Views of Pushkin's 'Eugene Onegin'*, Indiana, 1988.

The following works contain substantial materials on the novel:

J. Bayley, *Pushkin: a Comparative Commentary*, Cambridge, 1971.

A. D. P. Briggs, *Alexander Pushkin: a Critical Commentary*, Croom Helm, 1983, and Bristol Classical Press (paperback), 1991.

J. Fennell, *Nineteenth-century Russian Literature: Studies of Ten Russian Writers*, London, 1973.

R. Freeborn, *The Rise of the Russian Novel*, Cambridge, 1973.

H. Gifford, *The Novel in Russia*, London, 1964.

J. Lavrin, *Pushkin and Russian Literature*, London, 1947.

D. Mirsky, *Pushkin*, London, 1926.

D. J. Richards and C. R. S. Cockrell, *Russian Views of Pushkin*, Oxford, 1976.

W. M. Todd, *Fiction and Society in the Age of Pushkin*, Cambridge, Mass., 1986.

W. N. Vickery, *Alexander Pushkin*, New York, 1970.

The following works relate Pushkin's *Yevgeny Onegin* to Tchaikovsky's opera of the same name:

A. D. P. Briggs, 'The Blasphemous Masterpiece: Tchaikovsky's Adaptation of *Eugene Onegin*', Second Pushkin Lecture, Pushkin Prizes Trust, Queen's University, Belfast, 1994.

G. Schmidgall, *Literature as Opera*, New York, 1977.

The following articles, taken from the hundreds written about *Yevgeny Onegin*, will be found useful:

J. D. Clayton, 'Towards a Feminist Reading of *Evgenii Onegin*, *Canadian Slavonic papers*, 1987, XXIX, pp. 255–65.

R. A. Gregg, 'Tat'iana's two dreams: the unwanted spouse and the demonic lover', *Slavonic and East European Review*, 1970, LVIII, No. 113, pp. 492–505.

S. Mitchell, 'The digressions in *Yevgeniy Onegin*', *Slavonic and East European Review*, 1965, XLIV, pp. 51–65.

E. Wilson, 'The strange case of Pushkin and Nabokov', in *A Window on Russia*, London, 1972, pp. 209–37.

J. B. Woodward, 'The principle of contradictions in *Yevgeniy Onegin*', *Slavonic and East European Review*, 1982, No. 60, pp. 25–43.

TEXT SUMMARY

Chapter One
Lengthy introduction to Yevgeny Onegin, a young man of about twenty-five, who, after a rather superficial education, has spent eight years in St Petersburg society, living a life of idleness and dissipation. He inherits a country estate from an uncle, but, on taking up residence there, he finds himself no less bored and restless than he has been previously in the city.

Chapter Two
Onegin meets and apparently befriends a seventeen-year-old neighbour, Vladimir Lensky, who is in love with a local girl, Olga Larina.

Chapter Three
Olga's sister, Tatyana, obsessed with the heroes and heroines of sentimental literature, falls in love with Onegin, and naïvely offers herself to him in a long letter.

Chapter Four
Onegin rejects her offer and lives on in the country like a recluse. Months later he is invited to the Larins' for Tatyana's name-day celebrations. Lensky and Olga are now planning their impending wedding.

Chapter Five
Tatyana suffers a lurid nightmare in which she is first chased by a bear and then intimidated by monsters. Onegin comes to her rescue. When Olga and Lensky appear Onegin starts a wild argument which ends with him seizing a knife and stabbing Lensky. At the evening ball Onegin becomes angry with Lensky, who has led him to expect only a modest occasion. By way of revenge he monopolises Olga to an insulting degree; Lensky has no option but to challenge him to a duel.

Chapter Six
Lensky is shot dead. Within a few months Olga has married a hussar and departed. Onegin leaves the area.

Chapter Seven
Tatyana visits Onegin's castle, browses through his books and begins to realise what an insubstantial character he really is. Her family takes her off to Moscow, where the chances of marriage are better.

Chapter Eight
Almost three years later Onegin returns to St Petersburg where he meets Tatyana, now married to a Prince and occupying a high position in society. It is his turn to fall in love and declare his affection in a letter, but, at a final confrontation, she rejects him, saying that she will not betray her husband.

ACKNOWLEDGEMENTS

The editor and publishers wish to thank the following for permission to use copyright material:

Cambridge University Press for material from John Bayley, *Pushkin: A Comparative Commentary*, 1971, pp. 236–45; and Richard Freeborn, *The Rise of the Russian Novel*, 1973, pp. 35–7;

Harvard University Press for material from William Mills Todd III, *Society in the Age of Pushkin: Ideaology, Institutions and Narrative*, pp. 125–7. Copyright © 1986 by the President and Fellows of Harvard College;

University of Toronto Press for material from J. Douglas Clayton, *Ice and Flame: Alexsandr Pushkin's 'Eugene Onegin'*, pp. 139–43.

Every effort has been made to trace all the copyright holders, but if any have been inadvertently overlooked the publishers will be pleased to make the necessary arrangement at the first opportunity.

DRAMA
IN EVERYMAN

A SELECTION

Everyman and Medieval Miracle Plays
EDITED BY A. C. CAWLEY
A selection of the most popular medieval plays **£3.99**

Complete Plays and Poems
CHRISTOPHER MARLOWE
The complete works of this fascinating Elizabethan in one volume **£5.99**

Complete Poems and Plays
ROCHESTER
The most sexually explicit – and strikingly modern – writing of the seventeenth century **£6.99**

Restoration Plays
Five comedies and two tragedies representing the best of the Restoration stage **£7.99**

Female Playwrights of the Restoration: Five Comedies
Rediscovered literary treasures in a unique selection **£5.99**

Poems and Plays
OLIVER GOLDSMITH
The most complete edition of Goldsmith available **£4.99**

Plays, Poems and Prose
J. M. SYNGE
The most complete edition of Synge available **£6.99**

Plays, Prose Writings and Poems
OSCAR WILDE
The full force of Wilde's wit in one volume **£4.99**

A Doll's House/The Lady from the Sea/The Wild Duck
HENRIK IBSEN
A popular selection of Ibsen's major plays **£4.99**

£6.99

AVAILABILITY

All books are available from your local bookshop or direct from **Littlehampton Book Services Cash Sales, 14 Eldon Way, Lineside Estate, Littlehampton, West Sussex BN17 7HE.** PRICES ARE SUBJECT TO CHANGE.

To order any of the books, please enclose a cheque (in £ sterling) made payable to Littlehampton Book Services, or phone your order through with credit card details (Access, Visa or Mastercard) on 0903 721596 (24 hour answering service) stating card number and expiry date. Please add £1.25 for package and postage to the total value of your order.

In the USA, for further information and a complete catalogue call 1-800-526-2778.

EVERYMAN

YEVGENY ONEGIN

Alexander Pushkin

Edited and revised by A. D. P. Briggs
University of Birmingham

Based on a translation by Oliver Elton

The less we love her, when we woo her,
The more we please a woman's heart,
And are the surer to undo her
And snare her with beguiling art.

Yevgeny Onegin is disenchanted with life. A complex young man of purposeless leisure, he leads a turbulent existence of tedious sensations and endless social calls that serve only to bore him. Not even the innocent and sympathetic affections of Tatyana are able to rouse him. He lacks the heart to embrace love and can only pity her passion.

But as time inevitably passes, youth fast turns to age, and naivety to experience. People do not remain the same. Emotionally scarred by a fatal duel with his friend Lensky, Onegin learns the value of love. Years later, when he meets Tatyana again and love re-surfaces, it is on very different but equally negative terms.

A novel in verse, *Yevgeny Onegin* is the first great Russian work of fiction. Pushkin's love story is both earthy and tender, drawing with wit on the trials of life the poet saw around him.

The most comprehensive paperback edition available, with introduction, notes, selected criticism, text summary and chronology of Pushkin's life and times

Cover illustration: 'Man Reading by Lamplight', by George Friedrich Kersting (Museum Stiftung Oskar Reinhart, Winterthur)
Cover design: The Tango Design Consultancy

ISBN 0-460-87595-7

UK £6.99
USA $7.95
CAN $9.99